Morgan Lomax
To: Marion
Nov. 13, 2021

Broken Mirrors

Broken Mirrors

MORGAN LOMAX

DeedsPublishing | Athens

Published by Deeds Publishing in Athens, GA
www.deedspublishing.com

Printed in The United States of America

Cover design by Morgan Lomax.

ISBN 978-1-950794-31-7

Books are available in quantity for promotional or premium use. For information, email info@deedspublishing.com.

First Edition, 2021

10 9 8 7 6 5 4 3 2 1

This book is dedicated to my loving parents, Kirby and Sheila Lomax, who always supported me in pursuing my talents and dreams, but most importantly, this book is dedicated to God, Who gave me those talents and dreams to pursue in the first place. I could not have done anything without Him.

CHAPTER 1

It was the beginning of summer in a village nestled in a wood on the coast of England. Vibrant hardwood saplings timidly stuck their twigs out of the dense barrage of pines to catch a patch of sunlight while withering tufts of grass hugged the walls of shops and huts in a desperate attempt to escape the sweltering coastal heat. Lizards crept to the tops of rocks to bathe in the glowing warmth. However, they soon scurried away whenever the tramping of feet came too close, which happened quite often, for the whole village was bustling with activity. Summertime was one of the most exciting times of the year for the people that lived there because summer not only guaranteed time off from school but also an influx of visitors which the little village rarely received.

To welcome the tourists and entice them to stick their noses into their shops, everyone helped decorate the village and design stunning displays. Grocers arranged vibrant crates of fruits and vegetables from the early harvest in their open-air markets. Shopkeepers were busy repainting their signs and sweeping dust that had flown onto their mats from the street. Young boys were hired to wash windows and stock the newspaper stands with papers, magazines, and brochures about the village. Women planted colorful flowers in every garden and window to brighten up the place, and tailors patched up old vests and trousers and added a little embellishment to make them look brand new. Every flower-strung hut and rosy-cheeked villager glowed with the exciting prospect of summer. Even humble homes off the main road of the town celebrated this festive occasion. However, there was one cranny of the village that this excitement seemed unable to touch.

A wall of Leyland cypress trees isolated the top of a hill on the edge of the village from the rest of the inhabitants cradled in the valley below. This barricade of trees was connected to a dense wood that hemmed in the opposite side of the hill. Behind the trees, an electric fence encircled the hill in a crescent. At the front of the property, a section of the Leyland cypress trees jutted out at an abrupt right angle to hide an iron gate. No outsiders were permitted to enter through this gate. Even the mailman was prohibited from entering; therefore, the mailbox was placed at the foot of the hill. Inside the seemingly impenetrable fortress was an old house paneled in darkly stained cedar. Black shutters outlined heavily curtained windows, and a black door loomed in the shadows of a front porch. The wooden railing surrounding the porch had been painted a murky black as well. A cracked stone chimney seemed to force its way through the depressing roof that was covered in dark teeth-like shingles. The outward shell of the whole house was so dark that it seemed as if a cloak of shadows constantly draped itself over it to further conceal it from the outside world. But despite its gloomy appearance, the house and the surrounding landscape were surprisingly cheerful. To the left of the house grew a charming little garden that was partly enclosed by an ornate metal fence with ivy twisted all about its thin bars. Bees hovered over an assortment of bushes against the side of the house, and butterflies flittered about lilies, irises, hostas, and marigolds dotting the rest of the garden. On the edge of the hill parallel to the garden were more decorative flowers and bushes that lined the woods surrounding the hill.

Crouched beside one of the rose bushes was the gardener of this mysterious place. At first glance, this man looked more like a British colonist from an old history book than a gardener. He was dressed in brown chaps pulled over a bleached pair of stockings. A tan vest hung loosely over the billowing sleeves of his cuffed white shirt. Bronze maple curls adorned his head like a mess of wood shavings from a carpenter's table, and a twisted stub of a beard dangled from his pointed chin like the stubble on a goat's face. Jolly wrinkles smiled from the corners of his amber eyes, and long depressions like parentheses around his mouth were permanently etched on his face from the abundant smiles that so frequently appeared there. He was a kind and gentle man who loved caring for the simple beauty of nature. No matter how difficult the upkeeping of an ever-expanding garden became, he never complained, for gardening wasn't a chore to him.

A sweet tune vibrated in his throat as the gardener struck at the roots of stubborn weeds with his shovel. When the last prickly plant had been plucked from beneath the rose bushes, the gardener leaned back on his heels to inspect his work.

"There now," he exhaled as he wiped his sweaty brow, "doesn't look so much like a jungle in there anymore. Don't have to worry about those pretty petals of yours getting pricked by that crab grass now."

The gardener grabbed his shovel and stood up abruptly. He scanned the woods that fenced in his beloved rose bushes. "I remember seeing some saplings that branched off of these bushes just a little ways into the woods. I'd like to inspect them and make sure that the weeds aren't choking them out. Perhaps they even have a rose or two blooming."

Carefully, he waded through the low hedge of bushes that led into the woods. As he pushed his way through the last wall of bushes, the gardener found himself standing in a small circular clearing of the woods. It was a secluded, grassy patch lightly littered with a few stray leaves in the shade of the surrounding trees. *Perfect place for a picnic*, he mused to himself. He was about to push deeper into the woods in search of the sapling rose bushes when a startling sight glued him in place. His shovel fell from his limp hand and landed with a muffled thud beside him, but he didn't seem to hear it. All his attention was focused on the figure of a little girl that lay sprawled on the grassy knoll in front of him. In his state of shock, the gardener hesitated on what should be done. Was she unconscious or merely asleep? Was she hurt? Where did she come from? Simply running through every question that flashed across his mind wasn't going to solve anything, and if the girl was hurt, action needed to be taken at once. Shaking off his apprehensions, the gardener slowly approached the girl and crouched down beside her still figure.

"Hello?" he timidly asked.

No response. He repeated his greeting a little louder, but there was still no reply from the girl. A wave of relief flooded over him when he saw the gentle rise and fall of her chest. *She must be unconscious*, he concluded as he continued to examine her. Long blonde hair was draped messily over her face. Her clothes were smudged with dirt and had small rips in places where twigs or other sharp objects had snagged on the fabric. She had no shoes on her feet, and a few shallow abrasions were scratched on her thin arms and legs. *It doesn't seem as if the girl has any serious injuries*, he thought as he shifted to the girl's left side. Suddenly, the gardener gasped and jerked his curious gaze away from the girl. A pool of blood had been collecting on the ground beside the girl from a terrible gash extending from the shoulder to the elbow on the inside of the girl's left arm. The gardener slowly regained his composure and gazed back at the pitiful figure.

"She's lost an awful lot of blood," he murmured to himself. "There's no telling how long she's been laying like this."

He grabbed his chin and stroked his beard as he pondered on what to do. He couldn't just leave the poor thing here. He'd have to inform the master, but what would the master say? He couldn't just sit there pondering all day; he had to do something. Before he left to tell the master about his findings, the gardener pulled an old handkerchief out of his pocket and carefully tied it around the girl's tiny arm above her gushing wound. He hoped that this would act as a pressure bandage to stem the flow of blood until he could come back to her.

Satisfied with his work, the gardener grabbed his shovel and dashed up to the house as fast as he had ever run in his life. He burst through the screen door that led to the side garden and galloped up the stairs into an open doorway on the second-floor hall. A broad-shouldered man with slick black hair was bent over some papers on a desk in a shadowy corner of the dark room. If it wasn't for his pale skin, he would have completely faded into the shadows. He was dressed in black from his polished leather shoes to his button-up shirt. Formal white cuffs peeked out the ends of his sleeves, and a white scarf was tightly wound about his thick neck and tucked into the collar of his shirt. A long black cloak tied around his neck draped depressingly over the back of his chair like a funeral veil. This cloak seemed to engulf the man in utter darkness, but despite its gloomy aura, the man was never to be seen without its protective embrace.

"Master Marlow," the gardener gasped as he leaned against the frame of the door trying to catch his breath.

"What is it Felix?" Master Marlow muttered without turning around from his work. "And why are you breathing so hard?"

"I ran all the way up here from the woods, Sir," Felix replied as he finally calmed his breathing. "I was digging up weeds, you know, from around the rose bushes down by the edge of the woods, and…I found something."

"What?"

"A girl."

Master Marlow abruptly paused in his writings and slowly looked up at the wall in front of him.

"A girl?"

"Yes, Sir," Felix replied. "A girl."

The master said no more; he simply stared straight ahead, not even seeing the wall. Felix could tell that he was deeply troubled, and this unnerved him. To break the strained silence, Felix cautiously continued, "She's badly injured, Sir. There's a nasty gash in her arm. I don't know how long she's been lying there, but she's lost a lot of blood. And she's unconscious."

The master slightly turned his head in Felix's direction, but the distressed gardener didn't notice this pique of interest. "Oh! We simply must help her, Sir. I know how you feel about things like this, but…"

"Show me."

Felix looked up in surprise to see the master standing before him and gazing solemnly into his face. He would help.

When they reached the clearing in the woods, Master Marlow swiftly strode through the bushes and squatted beside the girl. He took her slender hand in his and felt for a pulse.

"Heart rate is fine," he mumbled to himself. He put

his ear against her rib cage. "Her breathing is good. No punctures or fluid in her lungs." He quickly sat up and mechanically examined her body as if he had done so thousands of times before. "No broken bones."

Moving over to the girl's left side, he gently examined her lacerated arm. It was a ragged gash that was spread open like the gaping mouth of a hungry lion. Blood flowed ceaselessly from its depths like the spring of a river. She certainly had lost quite a bit of blood. In fact, the master was surprised that the girl was even still alive. He leaned in closer as something glittering within the red slash caught his eye. Tiny fragments of something were embedded in the tissue of her arm, but he couldn't quite make out what they were because of all the blood that heavily coated them. He had never seen such a wound before and was quite perplexed.

"What could have done this?" he whispered gravely to himself.

Master Marlow pulled himself away from the confusing wound. There was no evidence that she had been attacked by an animal or a person, for there were no teeth marks, traces of fur, or scuffed places on the ground. However, there was a faint trail of blood splattering the grass and leaves of the woods behind her. Whatever had happened to the girl, she must have fled from the scene before collapsing here. But to make sure of this conviction, there was still one more thing that the master had to check. As gently as he could so as not to arouse the girl, Master Marlow brushed aside a few strands of the girl's matted hair to view her face. There were no injuries to disprove his hypothesis, but he was too distracted to take note of that. His serious expression melted into curiosity as he gazed at the girl's sleeping expression. He had forgotten what it was like to look at a strange face. It had just been Felix and him for so long that Master Marlow didn't realize how much unique beauty there was to be found in each person. She was so pale, so delicate. Her blonde hair seemed to enclose her tender face in a golden frame. But the youthful beauty was distorted by the pained expression in her creased brow. Even in her unnatural sleep she was suffering discomfort and fear.

Dark circles that sunk beneath her closed eyes made her face look even more pale and sickly than it already was. At the sight of all this beauty and pain twisted together in this agonizing scene, something stirred in the master's heart. Perhaps he could see this face again when it was restored to its original health and beauty. After all, she was still a child. Maybe. Just maybe. But the hope that had flickered in the master's eyes for a brief second was quickly extinguished by a renewed shadow of gloom that swept over his face. No. It was not possible. He could not hope to ever go there, for no friendly hand would be there to reach out to his own searching one. It was purely wishful thinking. He simply could not torture himself with such vain desires that he knew very well were never meant to be. After all, why had he secluded himself for all these years in the first place? No. It was better this way.

The master jerked his body toward Felix who had been expectantly waiting in the bushes behind him. "Go prepare the operating table."

Felix nodded and turned to go, but he hesitated and turned back to the master. "Do you want me to take the girl?"

"No, the blood will stain your clothes. I will carry her."

Felix turned and bounded toward the house. Wrapping his cloak around the injured girl, Master Marlow gently cradled her in his arms and followed Felix.

On the right side of a narrow hall to the left of the staircase in the house was a small room that resembled a doctor's office. A stationary table-like chair was immediately in front of the door. To the right of this table was a granite counter with a sink and an emergency eyewash station. Drawers and cabinets lined the wall. Four more cabinets were mounted to the wall above the counter to the left, and a floor-to-ceiling pantry sat to the right. All these cabinets were stocked with medical instruments, catalogues, and medicine. When the master entered the room, Felix had already lined the operation table with fresh sheets and had placed a plastic liner in a metal pan on a movable table next to the operation bed. Master

Marlow gently laid the girl on the bed before washing his hands in the sink and pulling on some latex gloves. He stretched a paper mask over his face and grabbed an assortment of instruments from one of the many drawers. After setting these utensils on the prepared metal tray, he grabbed a nearly empty bottle of clear liquid and a washcloth. He squinted at the contents of the bottle.

"Hmm. There's not much, but it will have to do."

He looked over at Felix. "Felix, I want you to soak what you can of the cloth in this liquid, but be careful not to breathe too much of it in. You'll have to pick some more up the next time you go into town."

Felix obediently took the cloth and began soaking it in the strong liquid while Master Marlow filled a small plastic tub with warm water. Once it was halfway full, he took the tub over to the girl's side. After removing the handkerchief tied around her arm, he dipped a dry cloth in the tub of water and began cleaning around the gaping wound. When all the crusted blood and dirt were wiped away, Master Marlow used the remaining warm water to flush out the interior of the wound. Each time he splashed the water into it, the girl moaned and fidgeted slightly. Afraid that she would awaken, the master cleared away the tub and called to Felix.

"Felix, are you done soaking that rag?"

"Yes, Sir."

"Alright. Come over here and gently waft it in front of the girl's face."

After a few waves of the cloth, the girl's whimpering and twitching ceased.

"You'll need to do that periodically during the procedure," the master advised as he picked up a pair of tweezers from the tray.

Felix set the cloth aside and shone a bright light into the wound to help Master Marlow see a little better. Using the tweezers, he plucked out one of the shards he saw in the girl's arm earlier. He examined it with a magnifying glass and found it to be a minute fleck of glass!

"So that's what it is," he mused to himself. "Interesting."

He laid aside the piece and prodded around for more. Once he was sure that no more specks of glass were embedded in the girl's arm, he pulled out a filled syringe, a small bottle, and two cotton swabs from one of the overhead cabinets.

"Bring me the antiseptic," he said.

Felix brought over another small bottle that contained hydrogen peroxide. Master Marlow dipped one of the cotton swabs into the bottle and rubbed the antiseptic in and around the wound.

Next, he took the other bottle, squirted its goopy liquid onto the second cotton swab, and rubbed the goo in a wide swath around the jagged edges of the wound to numb it. Felix cleared away the unneeded bottles as Master Marlow grabbed the syringe. He tapped on it twice before inserting the needle into the girl's arm. This would numb the deeper tissue to ensure that the girl felt no pain during the procedure.

"Hand me the sutures," he commanded.

After disposing of the empty syringe, Felix brought several long threads and a needle over to the tray. Master Marlow threaded the needle with the first thread and began closing up the wound. He worked swiftly with a steady hand and a meticulous eye. He was almost like a seamstress sewing up the last edge of a pillow. Precision was key. One loose loop could leave just enough room for infection to creep in. All the stitches must be tightly drawn and evenly spaced. It was a tedious process, but it was nothing a skilled doctor like Master Marlow couldn't handle.

After about twenty minutes, the last stitch was drawn taught and securely tied in place. The master and Felix began cleaning the workspace and clearing away the dirty utensils when soft whimpers emanated from the bed. The girl was beginning to wake up.

"Felix, waft that cloth over her again," ordered the master hurriedly.

Felix rushed to the counter and grabbed the cloth, but to his dismay, the remaining moisture had evaporated.

"I can't, Sir," he replied. "The solution has dried up."

Master Marlow was frozen in panic as he tried to think of a new plan. Suddenly, he dropped the supplies he was carrying onto the counter and stalked back to the girl's squirming side.

"We'll just have to work quickly then," he muttered as he motioned for Felix to bring him the gauze and bandages.

Placing a thick padding of gauze onto the freshly sewn wound, the master hurriedly secured it tightly in place with a sticky roll of bandages. The girl began to fidget so violently that he had to put a firm grip on her arm to wrap it with a final layer of cloth bandages. He had almost completely bandaged the entire wound when the girl's eyes flew open in alarm. Both the doctor and his assistant froze as the girl's fear-filled eyes darted from one man to the other. She was breathing rapidly and looked like a frightened fawn about to dart. Suddenly, her bulging eyes caught sight of her arm being tightly restrained by the doctor. Feeling as if she were being pinned down by an attacker, the girl uttered a terrified gasp, wrenched her trapped arm free from the doctor's grip, and dove to the floor.

Like a cornered cat, she scuttled away from the two men until her back collided with the cabinets beneath the counter. It was quite dark in the room, and now that she was a safe distance away from the strange men, the girl scanned the darkness for their menacing figures. Master Marlow had stalked around the table into the shadows out of her view; therefore, when he suddenly appeared before her, the girl gasped in surprise. She tightened herself into a quivering ball as the doctor draped a black quilt around her shoulders. The girl looked in surprise at the comforting folds now surrounding her before lifting her fear-stricken face. She was met with two glistening eyes peering out at her from a face shrouded in shadows.

"Don't be afraid," the doctor growled as he crouched before the trembling girl. "I'm only trying to help you."

Master Marlow abruptly sprang from the floor and marched out of the room with his black cloak whipping dramatically around the corner.

For a moment, both Felix and the girl stared in astonishment at the door where the master had vanished. Realizing that he was being quite rude to their new guest, Felix shook off his surprise and trotted over to the huddled mass on the floor. The girl scooted nervously away from him when he extended his hand to her.

"It's alright," he assured her. "Don't be scared. Come. I'll show you to your room."

After a moment's hesitation, the girl timidly grabbed the friendly hand. Felix pulled her to her feet and led her up the stairs. When they entered the hall on the second floor, Felix walked past two doors on the left side before opening a third. He motioned for the girl to step inside. After she reluctantly did so, Felix undid the bed and had her lie down.

"Now, get some rest," he said. "You've been through a lot."

As he turned to go, the girl sheepishly held out the

blanket that Master Marlow had wrapped around her. Felix surmised that she wanted him to take it.

"Oh, no, my dear. That is for you to keep. Master Marlow uses blankets such as that one for just such things. You see, blood won't stain black material. It's alright."

He smiled reassuringly as he paused by the door. "Good night."

The girl made no reply. She simply stared at Felix with wide and imploring eyes as he quietly closed the door. He understood. She was probably still quite frightened from the whole ordeal. She probably didn't even know if she could trust her captors.

Felix had just started for the stairs to finish cleaning up the operation room when he heard Master Marlow's voice call him from deep within a room. "Felix, come here please."

There was something in the master's tone that slightly unsettled Felix, but he ignored it for the moment as he entered the study that Master Marlow had occupied earlier that day.

"Shut the door."

Felix obeyed his master's command, but he was definitely starting to feel that something was very wrong. Master Marlow was standing hunched over his desk, obviously struggling with himself. The only light in the room was a solitary candle flickering on a corner of the desk. Felix almost felt as if he were at a funeral because of the intense gloom that stifled the air. He tried not to sound nervous as he broke the deadly silence. "Is...everything alright, Sir?"

His nonthreatening question was like a blazing spark. It lit Master Marlow's short fuse, and he exploded like a bomb. He rushed over to Felix almost pinning him to the door. His snarling face was mere inches from the frightened gardener's as he spoke in the deadliest hiss that Felix had ever heard. "She...cannot...stay."

The master's eyes bored into Felix's like molten nails. Felix didn't dare to speak or even to breathe while the master drove his message into him with frightening force. He had often been the victim of his master's rages in the past, but never to this extent. After what seemed like an hour, Master Marlow finally stalked away from him and began pacing the dim room. Felix imagined that if the master had been a cat, his tail would have been lashing back and forth in extreme agitation.

"I just can't do it," he continued. "I CAN'T, Felix. I won't be able to put up with this for very long. I promised to help the girl, and I have. I won't do any more."

"But, Sir," interjected Felix against his better judgement, "you can't just send the girl out on her own in her condition."

"I know that!" he snapped angrily. There was an uncomfortable silence except for the muffled thumps of the master's pacing feet as he pondered on what to do.

"Well, Sir," Felix began timidly, "if keeping the girl

here is such a problem, why don't we call the police? They would be perfectly fine with caring for her at the station. Besides, they have the resources to find the girl's family quicker than we could."

"No. That is out of the question. If we contact the police about this situation, they'll want to come here and investigate. Interrogate. Including me. As far as this village is concerned, no one knows that I even exist, and I would like to keep it that way. No one — not even the police — has any right to come snooping around here. I do not like it, but it is better this way."

Silence draped itself over the room once again. Master Marlow was doing his best to think through the situation calmly, but the more he paced, the more agitated he became. Finally, he resumed the conversation in a difficultly suppressed tone.

"I promised to help the girl. I have, and I will. But she cannot stay here indefinitely. I will not allow it. So, listen very carefully."

He stopped pacing and turned toward Felix.

"I will care for the girl until her wound is completely healed. As soon as that day comes, she's out of here…and YOU, Felix, will take her to wherever she belongs. Do you understand?"

"Yes, Sir."

Master Marlow yanked his cloak about himself and stalked back over to his desk. "Good. Nothing more is to be said about this. My mind will not be changed."

"Yes, Sir," Felix quietly replied once more. "Good night, Sir."

And he shut the door on the master and his troubles.

CHAPTER 2

That night, the girl had cried herself to sleep, partly because she had no idea where she was and partly because she had heard muffled yelling and arguing from the two men somewhere upstairs. Somehow, she knew that the argument was about her. Late into the night, she finally fell asleep, but it was a fitful sleep fragmented with nightmares. That morning, she sat up in bed and examined the room that was to be hers for a while. It had been too dark to make out anything more than the silhouettes of the furniture in the room last night, and even though the wooden blinds of the window were tightly clamped together, the few pale rays of morning sunlight that peeked through the slats were enough to brighten the dark room.

Heavy black curtains hung like bats from the dark mahogany frame of the window. Slightly faded black wallpaper embroidered in dark purple vines and swirls looked as if it were trying to reach out from the walls to ensnare the girl. The bed was covered in sheets and pillows of similar design and color. All the wood in the room from the flooring to the nightstand was a rich mahogany. Aside from the bed and nightstand, the only other furniture in the room was a small chipped table, a battered wooden chair, and a short chest of drawers.

Even though these few articles of furniture cluttered the small room, they could not seem to remove the empty feeling it contained. There was little décor to make it feel like a home. The walls were completely bare except for a few antique oil lamps screwed in here and there. That was another odd thing about the room. There didn't seem to be any source of electricity like that in modern-day homes. This room looked more like the bedroom of a young lady from the 1800s! The girl couldn't decide if it was more comforting seeing the room as it really was or merely guessing what its features could be in the shadow of night. But despite this uneasiness, the girl felt some sense of safety. After all, the man in the cloak had rescued her.

She looked down at her mummified arm. It was the first time that she had really gotten a good look at it. Gently, she ran her thin fingers along the whole length of the bandages. It was still numb. She cringed at the thought of what it would feel like when the medicine wore off and when she would have to remove the protective bandages. She hadn't realized just how large the gash was until now. Her entire upper arm was white with wrappings, and it had swelled considerably larger than her right arm. It didn't alarm the girl too much. After all, she had had stitches many times before. She knew the caring ritual by heart, and if the man who had doctored her wound was truly there to help her, she certainly had nothing to fear.

The morning light was growing brighter through the slits in the blinds, and the warm glow reflected off something smooth and shiny that caught the girl's attention. Resting on the narrow window frame was a bright red ladybug. Eagerly, the girl hopped off the bed and dragged the rickety chair over to the window. She clambered onto the wooden seat and smiled at the tiny crimson beetle. The little ladybug was vibrating her delicate antennas along the rough surface of the wood as if trying to determine what it was. Periodically, she would pause to clean her shiny black face by rubbing her tiny front legs furiously across it. Her oval eyes glistened like pearls in the early morning sunlight, and her vibrant shell sparkled like a ruby painted with black polka dots. The girl loved to watch miniature creatures. It was almost as if she had found a new friend. She giggled quietly as the ladybug eagerly felt the tip of her finger with her quivering antennas as if to say hello.

"Hey there," the girl whispered to the little beetle. "What are you doing?"

The little ladybug crawled onto the girl's finger and scuttled around in a circle. The girl's smile widened.

"You must be lonely in here by yourself. It must be nice to finally have a friend."

As if to reply, the ladybug nibbled on the girl's soft fingernail.

"I'd like to give you a name. How about…Rosy?"

The crimson beetle flexed her wings and zoomed back with a soft buzz onto the window frame. The girl gave a delighted laugh.

"Rosy it is then!"

She watched as Rosy scuttled along the windowsill. The little ladybug crept closer and closer to the blinds until she nearly bumped into them. As if in surprise, Rosy looked up at the blinds and began to climb them like a flight of stairs. She paused in a huddle when she reached one of the sunny patches forcing its way through the barrier of blinds. The girl's smile faded slightly as she watched the little ladybug soak up what sunlight she could.

"Aww. Are you trying to get to the sunlight? Don't worry. I'll take you outside."

She was just about to scoop up Rosy when the girl heard someone clear his throat behind her. Her back stiffened and her shoulders hunched in fear. She hoped that she wasn't in trouble. Slowly, she turned to face the source of the sound.

In the doorway stood the ominous figure of the doctor. She didn't dare to look up at his face. Even if she had, she wouldn't have been able to see his expression, for his black silhouette was completely shrouded in shadows. Neither moved nor spoke for a few minutes. Master Marlow examined the girl while the girl resolutely pretended to find something fascinating in the floor. Seeing that she wasn't going to speak or even acknowledge him, Master Marlow reluctantly broke the painful silence.

"May I take a look at your arm?"

Still without looking up at the doctor, the girl nodded, walked over to the bed, and sat on the edge closest to the door. *Well, at least she didn't try to run away from me this time*, the master thought moodily to himself as he knelt on the floor in front of her.

Willingly, the girl extended her bandaged arm out to the doctor. He gently grabbed it and turned it slightly in different directions to thoroughly examine it. He spoke not one word as he quickly went about his business. When he began to unwrap the outer bandages on her arm, the girl ventured a glance at the man's face. She couldn't restrain her curiosity any longer, and when she looked up, she was taken aback by what she saw. The man constantly surrounded in shadows was finally revealed to her in the morning sun. Slick black hair sat neatly combed back like preened crow feathers on his head. Malformed ears stuck out at odd angles from the silky locks. Two furrowed eyebrows formed a permanent crease in the middle of his forehead. Piercing eyes were tucked in the shadows of his thick brows. Dark circles hung like the heavy curtains of the bedroom beneath this penetrating stare. Over his right eye, a long, ragged scar extended from just above his eyebrow to the pointed tip of his cheek bone. Between his eyes, a long, crooked nose twisted its way down his pale face. A painfully large lump protruded unnaturally from the midst of that dreadful proboscis. Slashing across his scowling lips was another terrible scar that stretched all the way down onto his bulging chin. An unsightly black mole adorned this hunk of a chin as well.

Across his stern face and sunken cheeks, the girl could see strained lines caused by years of grief and misery. There were even stress lines protruding from his thick neck. Beneath the black cloak that always trailed behind the man like a long tail, the girl thought she saw a hump that caused the man's back to appear a bit stooped. But despite all these deformities and dark qualities, there was something about the man that intrigued her. She saw past all the ugly blemishes into something more. There was something handsome about this mysterious man. In fact, the girl even saw beauty in the blemishes themselves. Where did those scars come from? What was he trying to hide? She couldn't seem to pull her curious gaze away from his face. What was it that infatuated her so?

Master Marlow must have sensed her curious stare, for he abruptly stopped his work and glared into the girl's face as if to say, "What are you looking at?" For a second, their eyes met. The girl was startled by the intensity of his obsidian eyes, and immediately jerked her face away as it flushed a bright red. She hoped that he hadn't noticed. Turning back to his work, Master Marlow quickly finished rewrapping the girl's arm before springing to his feet and hurriedly stalking to the door without so much as a backward glance. He was about to disappear down the hall toward the stairs when the girl felt prompted to say something to him.

"Thank you ... for helping me," she shyly uttered in a mouse-like voice.

Master Marlow had to clutch the frame of the doorway to stop his lunging gate. For a moment, he seemed to be at a loss for words. He hadn't expected the girl to say anything to him. Soon, however, his shock collapsed into guilt. The girl's simple manners had struck a sensitive chord in his heart. He didn't turn to face the girl or even glance at her from the corners of his downcast eyes. He simply bowed his raven head as he rested his hand on the door frame.

"Think nothing of it," he solemnly grumbled in his deep voice.

He took a step forward. He was obviously anxious to leave the girl's presence.

"Wait," she called after him.

He jerked to a stop and leaned back into the doorway.

"May I leave my room?"

Master Marlow stood glued to the ground with his head still hanging for a second when he slowly raised it to look at the girl. There was still a stern edge in his expression, but something had softened its sharpness. Was it compassion? He spoke in a softness that the girl did not think was possible with his thunderous voice. "If that is what you wish."

With that, Master Marlow ducked around the corner and disappeared. The girl remained sitting on the bed listening to the doctor's long strides quickly fade away as he descended the steps. When she was quite sure that she could no longer hear his echoing steps, she sprang from the bed and rushed back to the window.

"Come on, Rosy," she whispered as she gently

prodded the little ladybug into her small hands. The girl slowly crossed the room while making sure that Rosy didn't fall off the edge of her palms. Upon reaching the door, she hesitated. Was it alright if she explored beyond the four corners of her room? The doctor had said she could, but she still felt a bit unsure. She worried that she might be breaking the rules. Cautiously, she scanned both ends of the hall. No one was there. Feeling slightly more confident now that she knew she was indeed alone, the girl stepped out into the hall and tiptoed toward the stairs.

When Mr. Felix had led her to her room last night, the girl had been too frightened and blinded by the dark to take much notice of the décor of the house. As she slowly retraced her steps that morning, the golden sunlight illuminated its strange features. The same gothic wallpaper lined the hall and the stairway. More oil lamps appeared along the walls, but the spaces in between were devoid of portraits and other decorations. In fact, it didn't seem as if any such niceties had ever even occupied the walls, for there were no nails or hooks jutting out. It was all rather sterile and uninviting, like a guarded fortress. Even the upper hall and stairs seemed dedicated to withstanding outside detection with their muffling roads of rugs.

At the bottom of the stairs, the girl noticed a small entranceway that enclosed a front door. There were no pictures there either. Turning to her right, she passed through a combined kitchen and dining space that was completely open to what seemed like the den. Two plush, antique-looking chairs faced inward toward a cold stone fireplace. An oval rug that matched the ones in the hall and on the stairs lay between the chairs. Ashes from a long-extinguished fire lightly powdered the wooden floor just in front of the fireplace. The fireplace itself yawned its cave-like mouth in a forbidding manner. Though she was quite repelled by this dark corner of the house, one thing did intrigue the girl. Almost completely concealed in shadows was a mahogany bookcase that composed the left wall of the den. It was stuffed with countless books. The girl was itching to see what kinds of books they were, but she didn't dare to go snooping around. She had this eerie feeling that she was being carefully watched, even though she hadn't seen any signs of the two men since emerging from her room. So, without any further exploration, the girl cautiously continued toward the open side door of the house.

As she neared it, she began to hear a faint melody floating in from outside. Pausing just inside the threshold, the girl curiously craned her head around the frame to see where the music was coming from. It was Mr. Felix, the gardener, humming a cheerful tune as he was pruning some low bushes in the garden that grew against the side of the house.

She continued to watch him as he merrily went

about his work when he suddenly turned and spotted her. The girl gasped and quickly ducked back inside.

"It's alright!" Felix called to her. "You can come out."

Timidly, the girl fully emerged into the garden, still cupping the tiny ladybug in her trembling hands.

"Come!" Felix said eagerly, inviting her closer. "I was just trimming up the garden a bit."

Feeling a little more confident from the gardener's friendly nature, the girl did creep a little closer and began to be drawn in by the beautiful flowers. Felix smiled at her shyness. As he gazed at the sheepish girl, his eyes wandered toward her cupped hands.

"What have you got there?"

Being pulled out of her wonder at the flowers, the girl jerked her head up in alarm. She realized that she had overreacted and immediately lowered her head in embarrassment. "Oh! It's a ladybug. I was just coming to put Rosy…"

The girl's quiet voice trailed away as her face flushed a deep crimson. Felix realized that she was embarrassed as he moved closer for a better look at the ladybug.

"She's beautiful. And you named her Rosy?"

The girl nodded her tucked head so hard that it knocked against her chest.

"That's a lovely name. Don't be embarrassed," he added. "I think it's nice to give things names. Why, I even name my plants sometimes."

The girl looked up at Felix and smiled at him for the first time. She appreciated his understanding. Looking back at Rosy, she decided to finish what she was going to say.

"I found her in my room, and I was just going to take her outside."

"Oh, I bet she'd like that," he agreed. "After all, this is where she belongs."

Stepping over to one of the freshly pruned bushes, the girl uncurled her hand to let Rosy crawl onto one of its leaves.

"Oh! Not on the azalea bushes! I don't want her to eat them."

"She won't," she assured him. "She'll eat these."

Felix followed her pointing finger to several miniscule green insects scurrying all over part of the azalea bush.

"What are those?" he asked in partial disgust.

"Those are aphids. They *will* eat your plants."

"Well then, by all means, Rosy, stay! Invite your other ladybug friends to join you as well."

The girl chuckled at Felix's urgent request and flailing hand motions to Rosy. He smiled back with a warm glow in his amber eyes. He was just about to resume his pruning when a thought suddenly struck him.

"Oh, my dear!" he exclaimed as he bowed to the bewildered girl. "I don't believe that I've properly introduced myself to you. I'm Felix Higginshire, Master Marlow's butler and gardener."

He twirled his hand and gave a slight bow of his head.

"Well, the gardening is more of a hobby," he added. "And what is your name, my dear?"

"I'm Alvera Levlen."

"Alvera. That's a beautiful name."

"Thank you," she meekly responded.

"How old are you, Alvera?"

"Fourteen."

"Ah, fourteen," Felix said in a reminiscent voice as he squatted down to dig up some weeds. "I remember when I was fourteen. Ugh! I was a wreck! But you'll be fine. You're not at all the pain that I was. In fact, you're probably the...oh dear!" he suddenly exclaimed as he slapped a hand over his eyes. "I do believe I've killed the poor creature!"

Alvera crouched down next to the horrified gardener and peered curiously into a hole that he had begun to dig around a particularly fibrous weed. His shovel lay next to a tiny gray creature that seemed to have been cut in half by the pointed metal blade. Reaching into the hole, Alvera scooped up the shiny ball.

"He's alright," she said. "Watch."

Still grimacing, Felix reluctantly looked at the tightly curled ball of gray that lay motionless in Alvera's hands. After a few minutes, the ball slowly uncurled to reveal a stubby armored body with hair-like legs. The gardener's eyes bulged in wonder.

"Remarkable! I've never seen such a creature before! What is it?"

"It's a pill bug. They curl up into little balls whenever they feel threatened or frightened. Their hard shells act like armor to protect them. I like to call them roly-polies."

"A roly-poly," Felix repeated still in awe. "Fascinating! Simply fascinating! What shall we name him?"

"Hmmm...how about...Shield?"

"Brilliant! That's a perfect name for him with all those armored plates of his."

"Would you like to hold him?" Alvera offered as she extended the tiny roly-poly toward him.

Felix immediately backed away and held up his hands.

"No! thank you, dear," he laughed nervously. "I don't do well with creepy, crawly creatures. You go ahead."

Resuming his gardening, Felix smiled as he caught glimpses out of the corners of his eyes of Alvera playing with the pill bug. Tiny Shield would crawl to the tip of her finger, slip as he lost his footing, and tumble down in a little ball back into her palm like a marble being rolled down a slide. She giggled every time. Eventually Shield tired of that game and resorted to simply exploring the rest of the girl's soft hand. As he crawled and wriggled about, Alvera turned toward the door without thinking about it. Suddenly, Master Marlow glided through the door.

"Felix…"

He stopped. Alvera found herself facing the menacing doctor. She lowered her head instinctively and pulled Shield closer to her. She didn't have to look to know that Master Marlow's stabbing eyes were glowering over her. The master had been just as surprised to find the girl out in the garden as she had been with his sudden appearance. Felix cheerfully greeted the stony doctor as if nothing were wrong.

"Ah! Master Marlow! Come out to get some fresh air? Good!"

He continued his gardening, knowing not to expect a response. And rightly so! The master was too preoccupied with Alvera to even notice Felix. He frowned at her disgruntled blonde hair that shimmered like an untamed golden stream in the sun. His piercing eyes followed the gold strands down to her waist until they were distracted by something else.

Master Marlow's unwanted attention was suddenly drawn to Alvera's cupped hands. He furrowed his brow deeper and cocked his head slightly.

"What are you holding?"

Alvera was speechless for a moment. The doctor had never engaged her like this before. Was he opening up to her?

"It's…it's a pill bug," she timidly stuttered before stretching out her hands for the doctor to have a better look.

Master Marlow's stoic expression did not change as he glanced down at the squirming crustacean. He stared as if in deep contemplation for quite a while before returning his serious gaze to Alvera.

"You like small creatures?" he asked. Now, Alvera couldn't believe her ears. Did she detect a subtle pique in interest? Lifting her head up slightly, she nodded. Master Marlow pondered again with that analytical scan pulsating from his eyes like a laser. He took a deep breath and exhaled dramatically.

"I'll get a jar."

He was just about to vanish through the door when Alvera called to him.

"No…thank you, Sir. I would love to keep him, but he needs to be free."

Squatting down, Alvera released the pill bug under a bush and smiled at him as he crawled away. All Master Marlow could do was furrow his brow once again. He was quite perplexed by the girl's actions. She certainly wasn't anything like he had expected, and somehow, he wasn't disappointed by this.

CHAPTER 3

L ater in the evening, Alvera curled up like a cat on her bed. The numbing medicine in her arm was beginning to wear off, and the dull pain seemed to throb throughout her entire body. She felt weak and drained and could not get comfortable, no matter what position she curled herself into. The pain was stabbing and felt as if it were ripping open her wound. That night, upon Master Marlow's order, Felix came and gave her some medicine that would hopefully block out some of the excruciating pain and allow her to rest. It helped some, but the fire in her arm would not be completely snuffed out. Alvera drifted in and out of a tortured sleep. She broke out in a sweat several times when the flames would flash across her whole body. At times when she began to shake violently, she wondered if she were battling a fever or some dreadful nightmare. She was too delirious to tell.

In the morning, Alvera opened her drowsy eyes to

another bright and clear day. The struggles of last night were still flashing through her mind like the agonizing pain that she had felt. Even her sweat still clung to her in a salty residue. She lay there slowly breathing and staring up at the ceiling. The pain of yesterday was gone, but a paralyzing soreness had been left in its place. Alvera was afraid that if she moved, the fiery pain would spark back to life. But she couldn't just lie in bed all day. If she didn't move her arm, it would become stiff.

Reluctantly, she decided to get up. She winced when she tried to push herself up with her left arm. The whole muscle felt like one giant knot of a bruise. Tucking her bandaged arm close to her side, Alvera pushed herself up with just her right arm. She took a deep breath and slumped a bit as she released it. She had forgotten just how uncomfortable and frustrating recovering from stitches was. Being in a strange home with two men she barely knew didn't make her situation any better. As far as she knew, there was no one there to comfort her, even though both men were willing to help her. She wished she were home, but she couldn't think about home right now. Definitely not now. Maybe not even ever again.

Alvera was spared from any more depressing thoughts by the opening of her bedroom door. Felix stepped in carrying a towel, a washcloth, and a small stack of fresh clothes.

"Good morning, dear," he greeted, peaking over the load in his arms. "Master Marlow would like you to shower this morning. It's been just a little over twenty-four hours now, so it's about time for your wound to be cleaned again."

Alvera hopped out of bed, and Felix placed the towels and clothes in her arms. Although she didn't like the idea of warm soap and water stinging her arm, she did agree that she needed a shower. The sticky film of evaporated sweat on her skin was starting to feel rather disgusting. Felix gave a cheery smile and prepared to leave.

"There's soap and shampoo already in the tub. Just gently wipe over your stitches with that smaller cloth I gave you. After you're done, get dressed...don't worry. I'll wash the clothes you're wearing. And Master Marlow would like to examine your arm to see how it looks before he rewraps it."

Alvera was going to ask Felix where the bathroom was, but he had already trotted down the stairs before she could get the words out. He obviously had a lot of work to do that morning. She supposed that she would just have to find it herself.

Timidly stepping out into the hall, she looked both ways. All the doors were identical. Every one of them was painted in black with dark silver handles jutting out. Alvera didn't like snooping about a house that wasn't hers, but she had to find the bathroom somehow. She decided to start in the hall where she was standing before heading downstairs. She looked to her left again. There was only one other door past her bedroom on the same side of the hall, and she had heard footsteps thump into it every night. It was probably another bedroom. Alvera supposed the same for the doors across from her. On the right side of the hall, there were four more doors. One of them had to be a bathroom. Making sure no one was watching, Alvera nervously tiptoed to the first door on the right of her. She grimaced when the floor creaked as she stepped directly in front of the door. Maybe no one had heard that. Hesitantly, she reached for the smooth silver knob. She had just grabbed it when Master Marlow suddenly bounded over the top stair into the hall. Alvera jerked her head toward him and froze. The most awful expression of wrath contorted his face. His startling black eyes bored into her like enraged carpenter bees. She was in serious trouble. She just knew it.

"What are you doing?" he demanded angrily.

Alvera jumped at his thundering fierceness. She began to tremble, but this time, it was not from a fever. Frightened tears began to sting her wide eyes. She forced them back by quickly squeaking out an explanation. "I was looking for the bathroom."

Master Marlow kept staring hatefully at the terrified girl. He didn't believe her. *You fool!* he thought in exasperation. *You never should have entertained such thoughts the other day in the garden! Look what has happened because of it! You cannot trust her! She's just like the others.*

Starting forward, the master stomped past the girl,

halted in front of the door opposite her bedroom, and jerked it open. He pointed aggressively inside.

"This is the bathroom. If you're going to use it, get in."

Alvera quickly obeyed the master's command. Once she was inside, she turned to face him. He lingered by the door a moment longer.

"Stay away from that door," he threatened in a low growl. "It's locked for a reason. It means, KEEP OUT!"

He slammed the door in her face and stalked away. The thunderous boom of the door echoed in her ears for a few minutes as she stood staring in shock. So, that door was kept locked. Why? What was the master hiding? Why didn't he want her near there? Alvera's curious mind was racing with millions of questions about the forbidden door, but she knew better than to go back to it. If the master had become that enraged by her accidental encounter with the door, she shuddered to think what he might do if she went to explore it intentionally for answers.

Deciding that it would be safer to put the mysterious matter behind her for the moment, Alvera turned away from the door toward the bathroom. The entire room was covered in pale green tile. The only source of light outside of two oil lamps on the wall was a window draped in frilly spruce-green curtains. A rug the same shade of green as the curtains was spread in front of the tub. The curtain pulled to the side of the tub was the same style and color as the curtains in the window as well. Opposite the tub was a short porcelain toilet tucked in a corner. An old-fashioned pedestal sink was to the right of the toilet. Aside from the antique décor, it was a normal closet-sized bathroom. However, one thing completely baffled her. There was no mirror over the sink! A mirror in a bathroom was a standard design in every home that Alvera had ever been to. All that was over the sink were four holes where it looked like a mirror used to hang. If there was a mirror there at one time, why had it been taken down? Had it broken?

Alvera looked more closely at the rectangular area. Several of the tiles had severe cracks in them. Even if something had hit the mirror and broken it, it wouldn't have caused this kind of damage to the wall without damaging the sink. Besides, a new mirror would have replaced the broken one by now. It all just didn't add up. It was very strange. Suddenly, a new revelation struck Alvera. All the time that she had been in the house, she hadn't seen one mirror anywhere. The missing mirror in the bathroom was no accident. But why?

* * *

That night, Felix invited Alvera down to dinner. Three place mats had been elaborately set with fine silver-trimmed china, matching teacups and saucers, glass goblets, ornate silverware, and black napkins. A midnight tablecloth clothed the mahogany table and hung nearly to the floor. Freshly picked roses fanned out of a crystal vase in the center. Their blushing hues seemed to add a youthful glow that lessened the formidable intensity of the darkness. Felix was just finishing up washing the cooking utensils when Alvera started pattering down the stairs. She tentatively paused on the last step. As if sensing her quiet presence, Felix glanced over his shoulder and smiled at her.

"Come on in! Come on in!" he encouraged. "We're just about ready."

Alvera slowly glided over to the table. When she reached the middle of the table, Felix politely pulled out the nearest chair for her and gently pushed her toward the table once she was seated. The two end chairs were reserved for Felix and Master Marlow. Steaming mashed potatoes, green beans, and chicken had already been heaped onto the plates, and the glasses had been filled with water. Felix was just about to sit down with a kettle of boiling tea when Master Marlow eerily appeared like a phantom from some obscure shadow in the house.

"Ah! Master Marlow," he warmly greeted. "You're just in time for dinner. Won't you join us at the table?"

The master stared unenthusiastically at the table with his beady eyes while clutching a book. Alvera slumped slightly in her chair. She felt sure that Master Marlow hesitated because of her. Tucking his book under one arm, the master stalked around to the other end of the table.

"I'll just take it upstairs tonight, Felix."

He grabbed his plate of food and goblet of water and climbed briskly up the stairs without another word.

Both Felix and the girl stared after his billowing cape until they heard the soft click of a closing door above. Alvera hung her head over her plate and stared with downcast eyes at the food that no longer seemed appealing to her. Felix saw the disappointment stamped across her face.

"Don't take it personally," he advised in a low voice. "It has nothing to do with you. That's just how Master Marlow is sometimes. I would know. I've lived with him as his butler for about twenty years now. Not once has he ventured outside of the fence that surrounds this place."

Alvera looked at Felix with inquiring eyes. She wanted to know more. Felix saw this curious gleam in her eyes and decided to indulge it a bit. He continued, "Of course, he wasn't always like this. In fact, it was in the village just below here where Master Marlow rescued me, just as he rescued you.

"I was in my early twenties at the time and in a pitiful condition. I didn't have a home or a job. I constantly roamed the sidewalks looking for job opportunities in the shops. Several stores were advertising for new employees, but they always turned me away because I was so dirty and ragged. I slept under bridges and makeshift tents at night because no one would take me in or offer me a temporary place to stay. I had no one. All I did have were the clothes on my back. I didn't even have any shoes. But I had gotten myself into that deplorable situation with my reckless behavior in my youth.

"As soon as I was out of high school, I basically partied and laid around all day. I had no intention of going to college, but I did want to get away from my parents because they kept hounding me about my laziness. So, I moved out. They weren't happy with my decision and told me that if I didn't get my life together, I wasn't welcome back. I didn't care. I went out, rented an apartment, and hopped from one job to the other trying to support myself. I barely lasted a week at each job I tried. I wasn't a very reliable worker. Soon, the rent payments began piling up. In a desperate attempt to pay off my debts, I started selling every item and piece of furniture in my small apartment until I had nothing left. It still wasn't enough. I couldn't afford to live there anymore. Once I was abandoned on the streets, I remembered my parents' warning. I instantly regretted my squandered time and horrible habits, but it was too late now. I had made too big of a mess of things to go back. It seemed as if I was utterly alone.

"It was late in the evening when I found myself tirelessly wandering the streets for a job again. The sun had just set, so it was beginning to grow dark. All the shops around me were snuffing out their lights and locking their doors. There would be no more job hunting for that night. I needed to find some shelter where I could sleep. I was shuffling along the edge of the sidewalk near the street heading away from the heart of the village. Suddenly, a car came speeding toward me. I tried to scoot to the other side of the sidewalk out of its way, but the car was hurtling too quickly down the road to give me enough time. The side mirror smacked my face with such force that it knocked me off my feet.

"As I tumbled backward, one of my legs stretched over the edge of the sidewalk and caught between the front and back tires of the car. A shockwave of pain immediately rippled up my leg after a deafening crack as the back tires rolled over my leg as if it were a speed bump. I scrambled away from the road using my arms before another car could whizz by. I was breathing heavily from the adrenaline and pain that coursed furiously through my body. I didn't dare to look down at my leg for fear of further panic at the sight of it, but from the horrible snap that I'd heard, I knew that it was badly broken. I couldn't get up to walk to the nearest doctor. Even if I had been able, I believe that I would have been too disoriented and panicked to find where I needed to go.

"All I could do as I lay there thrashing in pain was call for help. A shop owner was just stepping onto his front mat to lock up for the night. I craned my neck around from my awkward position to see him and called out to him. He stared at me for a moment before hurriedly clomping away in the opposite direction. I was dismayed, but I wasn't about to give up. Several people passed me on the sidewalk as they headed for their homes. I called out to each of them, but none of them stopped to help me. Cars continued to flash by, blinding me with their intense headlights. After what seemed like hours of desperately calling for help with no answer, I began to lose hope.

"No one had passed me in quite some time, and only a chance car here and there buffeted me with a gust of wind. I felt that same pit of loneliness settle in my stomach that I had felt when I had lost my apartment. No one was going to help me. A cold chill swept over my body as the night air began to cool. Perhaps I was going to be left there to die. I closed my eyes and roughly rested my head against the cold sidewalk. Might as well get some sleep since I was going to be there for a while. Suddenly, a dull rhythmic thud began vibrating through my head. At first, I thought that it was the beating of my heart pounding in my ears, but as the drumming grew louder, I realized with a surge of hope that someone was walking toward me. Circling around me, a man hidden in a cloak of black paused at my floundering side. Somewhere in the darkness above, his eyes were looking down at me. I wriggled on my back until I got into a position where I could look at him.

"'Please, kind sir,' I pleaded, 'please help me.'

"For a moment, the man said nothing. Suddenly, his deep baritone voice vibrated softly through the still night air. 'Will you let me?'

"I thought it was the most absurd question that I had ever heard. Here I was lying helplessly on my back with a broken leg. I had no money, no shoes, and no family to help me. I was in the most deplorable condition imaginable, and here this man was asking me if I would *let* him help me.

"Incredulously, I replied, 'Yes, of course! Please!'

"With my unbridled permission, the man squatted down next to me and set down a leather suitcase that he had been carrying. He opened it to reveal a plentiful stock of medical supplies. I was amazed. Of all the people that could have stopped to help me, I found a doctor that had everything I needed.

"He quickly examined my leg and fixed it in a splint. When he was finished, he closed his suitcase with a snap and helped me to my feet. He found a nearby bench for me to sit on. I was so grateful for his kindness that I felt that I had to express my gratitude somehow to him.

'Thank you so much, kind sir! I don't know what I would have done if you hadn't stopped by. Is there anything I can do to repay you?'

"'No,' he curtly replied. 'All I ask is that you return to your home.'

"'But...I don't have a home.'

"At that moment, I believe the doctor realized just how serious my situation was. I wasn't just a patient with a broken leg. I was a miserable wretch without a home or a family. He seemed at a loss of what to do for a moment, but suddenly, he stalked over to me and grabbed my arm.

"'Come with me,' he gruffly whispered. We walked at a surprisingly brisk pace out of the village even with the doctor supporting me. Through the thick darkness, I could just make out the silhouette of a small house at the top of a hill that we were quickly approaching. At the time, there were no trees or fences that blocked the house from view. I was soon to learn that those would come later. Once we reached the dark house, the doctor quickly ushered me inside the side door, slammed it shut, and locked it. He remained facing the door as he spoke.

"'What is your name?'

"'Felix Higginshire.'

"'Felix, I'm Malcus Marlow. You will be my butler. You will do whatever I ask you to do, including going to the village for anything I might need, and in return, I will provide you with a place to stay, food, and clothing. But…'

"He rushed abruptly up to me and threw back a hood that had been hiding his face. It was covered in two jagged scars, and a rather large nose protruded out in a crooked manner from the middle. He pointed to it while fixing me in place with a stern stare.

"'You are not to ask me anything about this,' he hissed in a deadly voice barely above a whisper, 'or about my past. You are also not to tell anyone when you go to town of my existence. Do you understand?'

"I nodded vigorously. Master Marlow then stalked away from me and replaced his hood back over his head.

"Since that first night, Master Marlow has revealed more about himself to me. Even a bit of his past. He even stopped wearing that black hood of his. But even after twenty years with him, there is still much that I do not know and do not dare to ask about. I have kept my promise, and I don't want to lose his trust by breaking it. He certainly is quite different, but once you get to know him, you'll find that there is a kind and gentle nature within."

Alvera marveled at Mr. Felix's story. He truly understood what she was feeling right now, for he had once been in her shoes. He had been buzzing with questions too, but as he subliminally warned Alvera in his story, he had to refrain from asking too many. She must do the same. However, there was one question that she simply could not escape from asking, but she wasn't quite sure how to go about asking it. Felix could read her puzzled face. "What is it, dear? I can tell you're thinking deeply about something."

Alvera hesitated to answer, but if she were going to ask, she had better do it now. "Well...I've just been noticing something...about this house."

"Yes?" he urged.

"Why are there no portraits or mirrors hanging on the walls?"

The encouraging smile vanished from Felix's face. It appeared as if he had been dreading this innocent question. But the girl deserved an answer, so Felix explained what he could concerning the matter. "Well, to be honest, dear, I don't quite know the answer to that myself. There used to be a few portraits and mirrors scattered around the house, but over time, Master Marlow took them down and put them away. I believe that those things may have something to do with his past. Now, I don't feel comfortable telling you what I do know about his past. If he wants you to know, I believe that he should be the one to share it with you. But I will tell you this."

He looked around to make sure Master Marlow

wasn't listening and leaned in closer to Alvera. "He has a very troubled past and is quite sensitive about it. Don't ask him any questions that might allude to it. He will tell you if he feels like it. But don't worry. I'm sure he'll warm up to you very soon."

After dinner, Felix led Alvera up the stairs to her room to tuck her in for the night. On his way back downstairs to clean the table, he paused in front of the master's study and knocked on the door. A muffled answer came from within, inviting Felix to come in. He quietly closed the door behind him. As he stood there, Felix's eyes fell upon a cold plate of food that the master had set on a small table next to the door. The butler reprimanded his master's back with a cold stare. "You need to eat your dinner. You've already let it get cold."

"I'm not hungry," the master mumbled as he continued scribbling on the papers before him.

"Well, you must eat something," Felix retorted as he approached him.

Master Marlow didn't respond. He kept his face steeply bent over his work, pretending not to have heard the butler's last remark. But Felix wasn't going to be rebuffed so easily. He cleared his throat loudly and placed a hand on the master's shoulder. "Our guest wished that you would have joined us downstairs."

The furious scribbling of a quill was his only response.

"You really should get to know her, Sir. The girl is

very kind. Incredibly shy but sweet. She's already opened up to me a little bit."

"Felix," Master Marlow said as he laid his quill down and looked up at him, "I know where this is going. I promised to help the girl and care for her wound until she is well. Then she must be returned to her own home. Don't expect me to do anything more."

"Oh, I won't, Sir. I won't. I'm just saying that a little company might make the girl's stay here a little more comfortable. That's all."

"Felix," Master Marlow warned.

"Alright, Sir. Alright." Felix knew that he had pushed his boundaries far enough and backed away. He crossed the dim room to the door and paused to look down at the tray of untouched food once more.

"Would you like for me to take your plate, Sir?" he quietly asked.

"Just leave it there for now, Felix."

"Yes, Sir."

He paused in the doorway. "Goodnight, Sir."

"Goodnight, Felix."

As soon as he heard the click of the door, Master Marlow stopped writing and stared thoughtfully at his papers. He was thinking about what Felix had said. *I did see some odd characteristics in the girl when she was in the garden,* he reminded himself. *But Felix is right. She is terribly shy. She'll never be comfortable around someone like me.* He pondered a bit longer. He had been lonely for many years, isolating himself from the outside world. And now part of that world had come to him. Maybe he could see what it was like through her eyes. Perhaps it wouldn't hurt to try.

CHAPTER 4

"And down that hall is the library, the laundry room, the operation room, and a closet," Felix concluded. Alvera had asked if she could walk down the hall on the main floor, and instead of giving her a straightforward answer, Felix had decided to give her a tour. "Well, I've got some cleaning to do, but feel free to visit any of those rooms you wish."

Finally, she was left alone with some time to herself. Felix was a charming gentleman, but he could be a bit too talkative at times. Slowly, Alvera lightly treaded down the lower hall of the house. Unlike its upper counterpart, this hall was not cloaked in a dark rug. Its wooden floor was left unsheathed for the rays of the sun to reflect upon and illuminate the majestic walkway. A window let this glorious light in at the end of the hall. It was the only window Alvera had seen that was not heavily curtained.

The first room on her left was the room Alvera had

most looked forward to seeing. It was the library. Her head swiveled in all directions as she tried to soak in the magnificence of the beautiful octagonal room. Gorgeous floor-to-ceiling bookshelves were the walls. Their ornately carved mahogany shelves were crammed with hundreds of books. Two open spaces on opposite sides of each other had oil lamps mounted over small chestnut tables. Beside each of the tables were plum colored plush chairs for reading in. Alvera had never seen so many books in one person's house. It was amazing! She walked to the nearest shelf and began scanning the leather spines of the books. Hardly any dust covered the books, and most of them were quite tattered and worn from use. Several of them were various volumes containing medical terminology, including a doctor's dictionary, a few anatomy books, incision manuals, and biographies on the lives of different doctors.

The shelf below that one was filled with mysteries, old novels, thick classics, and several thrillers. These books were especially worn. Apparently, the doctor had a similar taste in books as she did. The only problem was deciding which one to read first! Little did Alvera know that she was being carefully watched as she squatted down to read the titles of the books.

Lurking in the shadows of a closet door beneath the stairs was Master Marlow. He tightly wrapped his cloak about him like the folded wings of a bat to better conceal himself in the darkness as he took note of every move the girl made. She wasn't like most children. She seemed to enjoy the serenity of a quiet place where she could relax and be herself. That was something the master highly valued himself. Apparently, she also loved to read by the way she was meticulously studying the titles of the various books. Another thing they had in common. *Good*, he thought. *Perhaps that would be a good conversation starter.*

Finally, Alvera selected a book from the packed shelves, stood up, and began skimming over the back cover of it. Master Marlow couldn't tell which book it was from his distance. He craned his neck around the corner of the wall to try to get a better glimpse of the book when Felix came prancing toward him from the den. The master quickly withdrew back into the shelter of his corner. Felix had been cleaning around the house, for he held a feather duster in one hand. He reached for the handle of the closet door beneath the stairs to store the duster when he spotted Master Marlow's hulking figure in the shadows. The poor butler nearly jumped right out of his trousers in fright!

"Shhh!" Master Marlow hissed out of fear of being discovered by the girl.

Realizing who the figure was, Felix breathed a sigh of relief and crept closer. He gave the master a confused look. "Master Marlow, what are you doing, Sir?"

He signaled for Felix to lower his voice by putting a finger to his lips. He then pointed toward the library. Felix followed his pointing finger. When he saw Alvera standing in the midst of the room, he understood and smiled. So, the master *was* curious about the girl.

"You know," Felix began in a low whisper, "instead of hiding in the corner, you could just go talk to the girl, Sir."

"I'm merely observing, Felix. Nothing more."

Felix's smile broadened as he eyed the master. Forgetting to deposit the duster in the closet, the delighted butler went on his way, chuckling to himself.

Master Marlow waited until Felix was completely out of view before he decided on what to do. He was slightly annoyed by Felix's untimely appearance and sly intimation. Even if he was contemplating getting to know the girl better, he certainly didn't want Felix to suspect those ambitions. Just to spite the pushy butler, Master Marlow deeply considered abandoning his undercover operation, but he feared that his presence may have already been disclosed. After all, Felix had just been there, and the closet beneath the stairs was clearly visible from the library. The girl must at least have caught a glimpse of the butler's movement out of the corner of her eye. And if she should see the master exit from that location just minutes after Felix, she might become suspicious. Then again, she may have been too preoccupied with the book to have noticed the commotion under the staircase.

However, there was just too much uncertainty to know for sure. He couldn't bail on his plan now. It was too risky. If he were going to go through with it, it was now or never. Taking a deep breath, Master Marlow stepped out from his concealed corner and approached the library. Alvera was deeply engrossed in the summary of the book on the back cover. She had just finished reading it when the master crossed the threshold of the door. As she turned the book back over to read the title again, she suddenly became aware of the familiar clomp of feet walking across the wooden floor. She glimpsed the polished black shoes of Master Marlow slowly approaching her as she stiffened her slender body and lowered her head in submission. The master halted about two feet in front of the petrified girl. The room filled with a tangible silence. In the rashness of the moment, Master Marlow had forgotten what he was going to say. All he could do was examine the girl as he did with everything. She was scared. That was the first thing he noticed. Even though it stung to know that she was afraid of him, Master Marlow sympathized with the girl. He may not have shown it, but he was just as uncomfortable as she was.

But despite her obvious fear, the girl didn't dart away. She remained rooted to the ground. It almost seemed as if she were in a state of fearful respect. That was quite odd to him. The next thing the master noticed was the girl's hair. The long golden wisps hung freely about her bowed head like a pair of sheer curtains. They hid her fleeting face just enough to prevent others from seeing a clear picture of her but not so much to where she could not peer out and see fragments of others. In a way, it almost reminded the master of his cloak. The tips of the flowing hair gently brushed the edges of the book that the girl still clutched in her delicate hands. The book! That was what he was going to talk about! Relieved that his memory had returned, Master Marlow hurriedly thought of a question to ask before his thoughts deserted him again. "What book is that?"

Alvera was surprised by his genial question. She wasn't in trouble? Nervously, she held up the book and pointed to its title without lifting her head. "It's *The Narrative of Sir Arthur Gordon Pym of Nantucket* by Edgar Allan Poe."

"I take it you like his works?" Master Marlow continued with mounting confidence.

Alvera nodded. "I've actually read all of his writings. I had just never seen his only chapter book by itself like this before." She shyly added, "He's my favorite author."

"Mine as well," the master replied with wonder.

For the first time since the two had been in the library together, Alvera relaxed a bit and lifted her head off her chest. She didn't look directly at the master, but she looked high enough for him to see her innocent eyes. They were like an intense crystal blizzard, and they hit him with their full wintry blast. There was almost something mournful in them, and the force of their gaze pierced into his heart. The breath was almost sucked from him as the sadness shocked his chest. He felt that same unshakable feeling that he had felt the first time he had seen her lying in the woods. What was it about this girl that caused these dormant emotions to stir? His palms began to sweat, and his confidence dwindled. He was becoming too exposed. Too vulnerable.

No. He couldn't do this any longer without losing control. He had to get away. Averting his gaze, Master Marlow scanned the shelves of books for a diversion.

One book grabbed his attention, and he snatched it off the shelf. "Here," he said as he handed the book to Alvera. "If you like Edgar Allan Poe, I think you'll enjoy this book."

He waited for Alvera to start reading the outside of the book before quickly bolting from the room like a feral cat.

Alvera looked up in surprise at the master's sudden exit, but she was soon drawn back to the book that he had handed her. It was entitled *Beowulf*. She had always wanted to read this book and couldn't wait to get started. But her mind wandered back to Master Marlow. She was beginning to see the kind side that Felix had told her about. Perhaps the doctor was finally starting to warm up to her. Maybe she could do the same.

Later that afternoon, Alvera wandered back down the hall where the library was. As she passed by the operation room on her right, she saw something move. After a second look, she realized that it was the doctor. She hadn't seen this room in its entirety, for the last time she was in it, she had been unconscious and sprawled out on an examination table. Felix had told her that she was free to explore any room she wished down this hall. Perhaps Master Marlow wouldn't mind. Cautiously, she ducked through the doorway.

The doctor was busy sorting various clear glass bottles on the counter next to the operation table. He looked up when he saw Alvera's shadow darken the doorway. A mixed look of irritation and surprise crossed his face. "Can I help you?"

Alvera was startled by his sudden question. She hesitated before answering rather awkwardly, "Is ... is it alright if I look around? Mr. Felix said that I could ... but I can leave if I'm disturbing you."

The doctor's stern expression softened at the girl's polite response. At least she was considerate of others.

After a moment of consideration, the master answered, "Yes, that's fine."

He immediately focused his attention back on his work as if the girl were not even there. Feeling more confident and relieved now that she had received permission to stay, Alvera began walking around the doctor's small office. It was much lighter in the room than it was the day she had been rescued. Aside from the upstairs bathroom, this was the only other room in the house that wasn't covered in that oppressive wallpaper. However, it was similar in the fact that no pictures or other decorations hung on the walls. The walls were simply coated in a sterile grayish green that matched the color of the cabinets, and light gray linoleum padded the floor. Alvera slowly meandered over to Master Marlow. By looking at his plentiful cabinets, it was easy to see that the doctor had any and every tool he could possibly need to help a patient. Several questions were beginning to form in Alvera's curious mind. Without thinking, she suddenly blurted one out. "How long have you been a doctor?"

Alvera flinched as the last words left her lips. She had forgotten to heed Felix's warning about not asking any questions that might pertain to Master Marlow's past. To her relief, however, he didn't seem perturbed by her question. He simply looked up from his work to think of a response.

"I've been in the medical field ever since I graduated college, but I haven't been actively involved for twenty years. However, I still keep up my practice by reading up on the latest advancements in medical technology and medicine. As you saw in the library, I have several books on the subject."

Alvera was impressed with how knowledgeable Master Marlow was for not having been an active doctor for twenty years. Twenty years. That length of time certainly had been popping up quite frequently around here. As she curiously gazed at the clear jars the doctor was arranging, Alvera thought of another question to ask, but she quickly decided that it would be better if she didn't.

Instead, she said, "Do you think you could teach me a little about your practice?"

Master Marlow completely stopped in his work this time and turned to look at Alvera. His face didn't show it, but inside he was filled with a pleasurable surprise. It felt as if the master had a little apprentice standing eager to learn by his side. "Yes."

CHAPTER 5

It was early in the morning, and Master Marlow was still in his study. He hadn't slept all night. Ever since his encounter with the girl in the library the other day, he had been struggling with himself. Emotions that he had not allowed himself the luxury to feel for years were now surfacing and threatening to overpower him, and the master was battling them as fiercely as he could. He was beginning to have a deeper sense of caring for the girl, and he wasn't sure if he wanted that. Could he allow himself to relax back into the way things used to be? Was it safe? Was he safe? No. Yes?

Master Marlow leaned back in his desk chair with a groan. He began massaging his aching temples. It could have been the stress of his thoughts or possibly the fatigue from his lack of sleep that was causing his head to pound. Whichever of the two it was, he knew that the pain would not cease until he resolved one of his two dilemmas.

Just as his pain was beginning to subside, Felix clamorously burst through the door, sending a new wave of discomfort pulsating through the master's throbbing head.

Irritated, the master turned on Felix and spat out, "Felix, how many times have I told you to knock before you just come barging in here?"

"Oh! I'm terribly sorry, Sir," Felix quickly apologized. "It's just that…I've been looking for the girl everywhere, and I cannot find her! Have you seen her this morning, Sir?"

In his frustration, Master Marlow wanted to snap back, "Of course I haven't seen her, you fool! I've been locked up in my study since last night! Watching her is supposed to be your job!" But he thought better of it. Felix was already upset. The master didn't want to upset him further. So, instead, he took a deep breath to calm himself and replied with a curt answer.

"No, I haven't, Felix."

The poor butler was on the verge of hysteria by that time, but the master was too annoyed to feel any sympathy.

"Oh, dear! Oh, dear! I just don't know where she could be!"

"Have you tried looking in her bedroom?" Master Marlow suggested sarcastically.

"Yes, I have! She's not anywhere in the house! I don't know what to…GOOD HEAVENS!!"

"What?" demanded the master after he jumped in surprise from Felix's sudden cry.

"You're never going to believe this, Sir! She's all the way at the very top of a tree!"

Master Marlow turned to glance out of the window that Felix was gawking at. Sure enough, there was Alvera perched like a dainty little bird at the top of a tree, and she was reading a book. The master just shook his head and turned back toward his desk. But Felix was not so amused by the situation.

"What should we do, Sir?"

"Nothing."

"Nothing!?"

"If she got herself up there, she can get herself down. Besides, she's just enjoying herself."

"Well, I certainly don't see anything enjoyable about it. Someone needs to talk that girl out of doing such dangerous things."

An idea flashed in Master Marlow's eyes. That was it. It was the perfect opportunity. No more battling with himself. Abruptly rising from his chair, he whisked toward the door.

"Where are you going, Sir?"

"Don't worry about it, Felix. Just go get started on breakfast."

Felix just stared after the master after he had long since vanished down the hall. He was more confused than ever.

Master Marlow plunged outside, taking long strides toward the tree. His cloak flapped like the wings of a crow in the refreshing summer breeze. When he arrived at the base of the tree, he looked up its smooth gray trunk. It was a towering poplar tree. The girl had to have been at least twenty feet up in its spindly branches. He could barely see her through the thick clusters of broad leaves and the painted orange and yellow blossoms scattered throughout the tree. She obviously had not seen him either, so he decided to call to her. He was going to call her name, but the master suddenly realized that he didn't even know what her name was! Ashamed at the realization, the master quickly thought of something else to say. "Hello?"

The unthinkable happened. The girl had been so startled by the master's call that she lost her balance and began to tumble out of her perch. Just as she was about to crash through the several feet of pointed branches below her, she caught hold of one of the branches that she had been sitting on and jerked to a stop. She uttered a shrill cry when the tug of her falling body yanked on her injured arm. Master Marlow looked up in alarm at her cry just in time to dodge the book that had slipped from her hands. It landed next to him with a flutter of pages and a thud.

He looked back up from the book to see the girl dangling like a flag from the uppermost branches of the massive poplar. Her breathing was almost in sync with her racing heart. Slowly, she calmed herself and clambered back down the tree. As soon as her feet touched the mossy grass below, Master Marlow rushed over to her and began removing bits of twigs and leaves that were caught in her flowy hair.

"I'm so sorry! I didn't mean to startle you like that. Are you alright?" He knelt down in front of her and held her by the shoulders as he looked earnestly into her bowed face. The girl quietly nodded. Then, she raised her head slightly, revealing a sliver of her aquamarine eyes before she lowered it again.

"I'm sorry about the book."

The master was surprised for a moment. Of all things, she was worried about him being upset over a slightly damaged book? He shook his head. "Don't worry about the book. I'm just glad that it wasn't you that fell."

The girl lifted her head a little higher.

"May I see your arm?"

Alvera nodded and held out her injured arm willingly. Master Marlow carefully unwound the bandages and examined the girl's wound, just as he did every day. Satisfied that the near fall had not pulled any of the stitches loose, the doctor gently packed the wound and wrapped new bandages back around it.

Standing up, he walked over to the disheveled book, dusted it off, and handed it back to Alvera. "Here you go."

"Thank you," she whispered as she timidly received the battered book. "I just finished it. It was very good."

"I'm glad you liked it."

A more serious look suddenly shadowed Master Marlow's face, despite the morning sunlight that filled the yard with a warm glow. "Let's go for a walk," he solemnly invited.

Alvera obediently followed the doctor as he started across the sea of soft green that waved lazily in the breeze.

Everything was so beautiful and peaceful. The petals

of the flowers blazed forth their more vibrant colors in the glow of the sun. Waxy leaves glittered with a golden guild, and butterflies fluttered through the air like flying streaks of rainbows. Songbirds chirped merrily from the swaying boughs of the trees. The same mellow sea breeze that rocked the trees was also wafting its saline scent along with the sweet perfumes and nectar of the blooming flowers. The aromas were so soothing that they seemed to put the surrounding nature into a relaxing sleep. Alvera felt as if she could lay in a sunny patch on the ground and daydream all day. She loved the outdoors.

The doctor and Alvera had made their way to the edge of the woods and were leisurely walking in its cooling shade. The only sound besides the music of the songbirds was the soft humming of bumblebees as they flitted in and out of the bushes. Suddenly, the tranquil silence of the woods was broken by the rumbling tones of Master Marlow's voice. "I asked you to walk with me because I wanted to talk to you."

Alvera looked up at the back of the doctor's head and listened carefully to his words.

"When I took you in, I only did so grudgingly. Please don't think terribly of me, but I really didn't want to. I haven't been around other people in twenty years, and I wasn't sure if I could handle it. But now...I see that I have sorely misjudged you. I've been a terrible host. I haven't been kind, inviting, or anything to you;

why, I haven't even bothered to ask you your name, let alone tell you mine."

Master Marlow had stopped, and the two were facing each other. Instead of Alvera avoiding his gaze, it was the master that was avoiding hers. As she gazed up at him with her big watery eyes, all she could feel for him was pity. She was not angry or upset with Master Marlow for the way he had treated her. She simply wanted to know why he was the way he was. But the doctor had just revealed a vulnerable side of himself to her. She didn't want to overextend her boundaries. That answer would come in due time.

Still looking up at his hulking figure, she said, "Alvera."

"What?" he asked looking curiously at her.

"My name is Alvera."

"Well," he stuttered, "it's nice to finally meet you, Alvera. I'm Malcus Marlow."

"Nice to meet you, Mr. Marlow," Alvera replied with a short curtsy.

The master looked back at the sweet girl. A huge smile was spread across her youthful face, and it was the face that the master had envisioned the first time he had seen her. Her delicate skin had regained its color as evidenced by a soft rosy blush that rested on her cheeks. No more dark circles hung beneath her eyes, and the hollow look of malnutrition that had been engraved in her face had been restored to its healthful resilience. Her vividly blue eyes sparkled with even more vitality, and kindness seemed to radiate from them. The doctor realized that she held no grudges against him for the way he had treated her. She only looked at him with … was it love? He didn't know, and he didn't care. All that mattered was that she wasn't afraid of him. Master Marlow was so overwhelmed with joy that for the first time in more than twenty years … he smiled!

CHAPTER 6

Over the next few days, the doctor and Alvera got to know each other a little better. At first, they each sat in a plush chair in the library and read silently together. Whenever they finished their books, they often asked each other questions and discussed the stories they had read. It was a comfortable way for the two to slowly build a friendship.

Soon, the master began joining Alvera on her excursions outside. Both would sit side by side in the grass beneath the poplar tree. Sometimes they would read in their shady seats, and other times, they would simply lean back against the smooth trunk of the poplar and enjoy the beauty of nature that stirred all about them. Little did Alvera know it, but she was slowly nudging Master Marlow out of his reclusive shell. He didn't feel as if he had to keep himself so guarded anymore. He found that conversation was beginning to flow more easily and naturally whenever he was around Alvera, for she didn't judge him as he had been judged by so many in the past. It was as if she understood him, even though she knew almost nothing about his history. He was discovering a new perspective of the world he once viewed as cruel from the kindness of this little girl.

True to his word, Master Marlow began teaching Alvera about his practice. At first, he simply told her the names of each of the tools that he used most often and what they were used for. He would then point to each of the instruments, and Alvera would have to tell him what each one was. She had more difficulty in telling what each instrument was used for than in naming them, but Alvera was eager to learn. She was fascinated by all the knowledge and experience that Master Marlow had, and even though she knew that she would never be an expert in the medical field like he was, she still wanted to learn everything she possibly could about the profession. Perhaps one day it might come in handy!

When Master Marlow was quizzing Alvera once again on different medical terms, Alvera spotted a young squirrel sprawled out in the grass. She rushed out to the poor squirrel with Master Marlow trotting close behind. After a thorough examination, the doctor concluded that the squirrel had a slight fracture in one of his hind legs, along with a fairly deep gash close to it. The squirrel had obviously been attacked by some other animal. The master was no veterinarian, but he certainly knew the basics of stitching up a wound and placing a

broken bone. When the squirrel first woke up from the procedure, he was extremely timid and afraid. He even attempted to gnaw off his little cast!

But after several days of gentle coaxing from Alvera, the young squirrel was soon quite tame. Everyone, including Felix, absolutely adored the little squirrel. He became the house pet and was dubbed Scamper. That name certainly suited the energetic rodent well, for he was often seen as a blur of gray fur zooming in circles around the house. He would eat from their hands and even perch on their shoulders. Scamper especially enjoyed riding atop Felix's shoulders when he was gardening, much to his discomfort!

Finally, however, it was time to release Scamper

back into the woods, for his leg had completely healed. Master Marlow had already removed the last of the stitches from the little squirrel's leg. All that was left was the cast. The master had recently started teaching Alvera how to perform certain medical procedures; for practice, he allowed her to remove Scamper's cast. He watched as Alvera carefully unwrapped the fabric bandage from around the hard shell of the cast. She set the cotton wrappings aside on a small tray that contained three instruments. The master drew her attention to them. "Alright. Tell me what this one is."

"It's a vaccination needle and syringe."

"Yes. What's this one?"

"That is a pair of forceps."

Master Marlow nodded before pointing to the last remaining item to be named. "Now, what about this one? Is it a bottle, or is it a beaker?"

Alvera contemplated the glass container for a moment. This was a tricky one. Finally, she had her answer. "It's a beaker."

"Very good. You got that one right this time. Bottles and beakers are very similar, but in my opinion, there is a difference."

Alvera smiled in amusement as she focused her attention back on the little squirrel and began cutting open his tiny cast.

"I remember when I taught Felix about the doctoring practice," Master Marlow mused as he continued

to watch Alvera in her work. "He was eager to learn just as you are, but he was not nearly as fast a learner. There was so much besides the medical field that I had to teach him. I almost pitied the poor fellow, but my frustration in trying to teach him prevented me from doing so." The doctor paused with a sigh. "But don't get me wrong. I am very grateful for Felix. He's been a great help and company to me all these years. In fact, if it weren't for Felix, I'd probably be living off cold cereal and sandwiches. I cannot cook at all. That was the one thing I didn't have to teach him. Felix is a master in the kitchen. I'm surprised he never aspired to become a professional chef."

It was so nice to listen to the master talk. For the first time, Alvera felt as if she didn't have to start up a conversation and keep it going. That was always quite difficult for her. She was glad to be able to just listen.

Scamper rubbed his fuzzy head against Alvera's gentle hand as soon as she had removed the cast. His bushy tail bristled with the same excitement that sparkled in his black marble eyes. Master Marlow looked up at Alvera with a thin smile. "Are you ready?"

She nodded and picked up the squirming squirrel. Both the master and Alvera walked out the side door and past the garden to the open yard. Squatting down in the shade of the ornate fence of the garden, Alvera lowered the eager squirrel to the ground. As soon as she released her gentle grip, Scamper leaped across the carpeted lawn of green. He looked like a little kid frolicking through the waving straw of a meadow. She smiled as she watched Scamper bounce around one last time before darting up a tree on the edge of the woods.

Master Marlow had also been watching Scamper, but now his gaze returned to Alvera. He knew how much she loved the little squirrel, and he marveled at how easily she let him go. It had to be a bittersweet parting for her. Although he was still a bit confused about setting things free, the master was beginning to understand this freedom as it slowly blossomed within him.

* * *

The next day, Alvera decided to help Felix with his chores around the house. She was tired of feeling like a burden to her two rescuers. She hadn't been able to do much with her injured arm, but now that it was really beginning to heal up, Alvera wanted to show her appreciation for everything Felix and Master Marlow had done for her. Besides, the master was busy working in his office that day. Helping Felix would give her some company.

"Thank you so much for all your help today!" Felix exclaimed as the two headed in for the evening. "You've been an excellent little helper."

Alvera slightly turned her head away as a soft blush

colored her cheeks. "Is there anything else you need me to do?"

"Oh, no, no, no! You've already done plenty to help me. I don't want you to tire your arm with anymore work. Why don't you run along upstairs and rest a bit? I'll put these tools away."

Felix paused and squinted at the pile of gardening tools stacked in his arms. "Wait a minute. Oh, dear. I knew I was forgetting something. Alvera, if you don't mind, I think I left a small bucket on the windowsill in your room when I was planting flowers outside the window this morning. Do you think you could run upstairs and get it for me?"

Nodding eagerly, she bounded up the stairs like a spry little fawn. Felix chuckled to himself as he turned toward the kitchen sink to wash off his gardening tools before putting them away. As he did so, the gardener spotted the little bucket next to the sink that he had told Alvera to fetch. He quickly turned back toward the stairs.

"Never mind, Alvera. It's..." but she had already vanished up the stairs. Felix shook his head in dismay and returned to the sink.

"Oh, well. She'll figure it out."

Alvera was already almost halfway down the upper hall when Felix had called to her. She hadn't heard him. She was too focused on her mission. Her bedroom door had been pushed closed to where only a sliver of

light peeked out into the hall. She figured that Master
Marlow must have come walking down the hall and decided to close it. Swinging the door the rest of the way
open, Alvera skipped inside. As soon as she was over the
threshold, however, she stopped in her tracks as if she
had been frozen to the spot. This was not her room. In
fact, she had never even seen this room before. Suddenly,
a startling realization caused her heart to race in alarm.
This was the forbidden room! Master Marlow always
kept it locked up tight, and here she was standing in the
doorway. *You need to get out of here right now!* her conscience warned her. *Wait!* said another part of her. *This is
your chance to find out more about Master Marlow.* It was
true. Ever since the master had warned her not to go
near this room, Alvera had been intensely curious as to
what could be lying behind the locked door. She took a
faltering step forward. *What are you doing!?* she yelled at
herself. *You're going to get caught! It's alright,* she reasoned.
I'm just going to take a quick look around, and then I'll leave.

As she cautiously inched her way further into the
room, Alvera knew that she should turn around, but she
didn't. She listened to her curiosity instead. Half of the
room was covered in the same dark wallpaper that the
rest of the house was clothed in. Deep chestnut-colored
boards lined the bottom of the wallpaper, and pale pink
carpet cushioned the floor. There was no furniture, but
Alvera was greatly surprised by the décor of the room.
To her left, she saw a collage of portraits clustered

together on the wall. She turned in amazement to find that the clutter of pictures extended all the way to the wall where the door was. Most of the pictures were in black and white, but there was one picture in color that caught her attention.

She crept closer to it. It was a picture of a small boy with rich black hair neatly combed over his head. He had a surprisingly large nose for a boy his size. She squinted at his unsmiling face. There was something familiar about him. Still facing the door, Alvera looked to her left. A pile of cedar trunks was nestled in the corner. A few of them looked as if they were about to burst from all the papers sticking out of the cracks in their lids. Other trunks had small fragments of glass strewn about them. Alvera was puzzled. These trunks obviously held some of Master Marlow's personal items, but what were the shards of glass about? She turned back around and walked deeper into the strange room and became even more perplexed by what she saw next.

The other half of the room was completely encased in floor-to-ceiling mirrors. Mirrors! Alvera hadn't seen a single mirror in the entire house until now. This was very odd. She inched closer. Several of the mirrors had extensive cracks that plummeted down the entire length of the panels. Others had thinner cracks clustered together in circles that resembled spider webs. Huge chunks of mirror from some of the deeper cracks were missing, and several smaller shards were sticking up from the carpet. Alvera began to wonder if the trunks with glass around them had anything to do with these mirrors. She didn't want to investigate any further. Everything about the room was extremely unnerving.

She took a step to go but suddenly froze like a statue. Her eyes grew as big as baseballs as she stared into the depths of the mirrors. Reflected in their silvery surfaces was Master Marlow's dark figure standing in the doorway. A deep scowl was scrawled across his scarred face, and his nostrils flared like an angry bull's. Alvera was petrified with fear. There was nowhere for her to run or hide. She was completely exposed and in deep trouble.

A flood of shame washed over her terrified body and seemed to melt its frozen position. With bowed head and tightly clasped arms, Alvera slowly turned toward the angry master preparing herself for severe punishment.

"What are you doing in here?" he asked through clenched teeth.

Alvera didn't look up. She couldn't. All she could do was answer in a quavering voice.

"I'm sorry. I...I thought that this was my room. I didn't realize it until I was in here, and..."

"And you should have turned around right when you realized your mistake," snapped the master cutting her off. "But you didn't. You just had to know what was in here. Didn't you? Do you know why? Because you're curious."

Master Marlow stepped into the room.

"You know what they say about curiosity? Curiosity...killed...the cat."

Alvera's heart was racing. She was beyond scared now. As much as she didn't want to, she timidly moved toward the door where Master Marlow was.

"I'm sorry. Please. Just let me leave."

"Oh, no," he hissed darkly sliding back to the door and closing it. "You've seen too much. You want to know why there are no portraits in the house. You want to know why there are no mirrors. You want to know why

I have these hideous markings on my face. You want to know why I haven't been an active doctor all these twenty years. Yes," he clarified when he saw the look of surprise on Alvera's face, "I overhead your conversation with Felix. I've heard much more than you realize."

He stalked like a prowling fox glaring malevolently at her the entire time. "You want to know why I have this room?" he whispered angrily into her ear. "This room serves as a reminder of why I hid myself from the world and why I can never go back."

The master roughly grabbed her by the shoulders and shoved her toward the portraits hanging on the walls. Alvera's entire body was trembling in terror. Thinking that she might have been trying to free herself from him, Master Marlow tightened his pinching grip on her tense shoulders.

"Look," he demanded as he lowered his face next to Alvera's.

Not wanting to infuriate the master further, she raised her wobbling head as quickly as she could. She didn't dare to take her eyes off the pictures. Their stern faces were much kinder at the moment than Master Marlow's was.

"What do you see?"

"I ... I see ... portraits."

"Yes, but there is more. These faces tell a story. A story of heartache as you can see by the expressions on their faces."

Master Marlow released his painful grip and stalked over to the cluster of portraits next to the door. He pointed to one small oval frame and looked sharply like a hawk at Alvera. It was the same boy that she had looked at only moments before.

"You see this boy? This boy is the cause of this family's problems because he was different. He was unloved and rejected ... even by his own father!"

Despite being even more terrified by the master's horrible snarl that wrinkled his face, Alvera finally understood. That boy was Master Marlow! And the rest of the portraits were all pictures of his relatives. The relatives who apparently hated him. Alvera saw nothing exceedingly out of the ordinary about the young Master Marlow. What could have caused his family to reject him? She jolted as the master continued.

"They abandoned me, so I have abandoned them. I never want to see their sneering faces again! Yet, I force myself to look at them ... almost every day because they remind me never to go back. They were not there for me then, so why should I expect anything different now?"

For a moment, the master was distracted by his brooding over unpleasant childhood memories. He was very unstable emotionally, like a lit stick of dynamite. Any moment, he could explode. Alvera didn't think she could take that. She had to get out of there, and now was her chance. She eyed the door. It was only about three feet away. She could make it. But before she could carry out her desperate plan, Master Marlow caught her eyes roaming over to the door.

"DON'T EVEN THINK ABOUT IT!"

Just as she had feared, the master's fuse had finally reached its end but not when she had expected it. Alvera shrunk about a foot as Master Marlow stormed over to her and clamped back down on her sore shoulders with that deadly grip again.

"I'm not finished yet, and neither are you! There's still one more thing you want to know. Isn't there!? ISN'T THERE!!? ANSWER ME YOU INSOLENT CHILD!!!"

Alvera gasped as the master's grip tightened even more. It felt as if it would surely crush her bones. "Stop! Please! You're hurting me!"

"Oh, this is nothing, my dear," he retorted cruelly without lessening his grip. "This is only pain. It will pass after a while. What I am afflicted by is torture, and tor-ture never stops. There is nothing like the wound of be-trayal, and even as we speak ... a new wound is forming!"

Jerking her around, the master thrust Alvera toward the mirrored side of the room.

"Look!"

Alvera couldn't look up. She couldn't look at the master's hate-filled face any longer.

"LOOK!!"

She jerked her head up this time.

"Now, what do you see?"

For several minutes, Alvera had been fighting as hard as she could to keep tears from spilling over. Now, she did not trust her inward strength. She could feel it beginning to falter. The only way to keep the tears back now was by breathing faster.

In between two rapid breaths, Alvera whispered, "A reflection?"

"NO!!" the master bellowed. "I see a man. A broken man just like these mirrors. A man cut off from the world just as these scars cut off my skin. A man deformed and despised by his closest family. A man transformed into a…a…A MONSTER!!!"

He slammed an angry fist into one of the undamaged panels. The silvery glass shattered into needle-thin shards that pierced his skin. Thin trails of blood flowed from the master's clenched hand into the cracks. Both were breathing hard. Alvera panted out of fear, and Master Marlow out of pain. But which pain it was, Alvera couldn't be sure of. Suddenly, he turned his head slightly toward the terrified girl. Alvera expected another harangue to erupt from his thin lips, but instead, she was met with a gruff whisper.

"Get out."

She didn't have to be told twice. Spinning around, she bolted from the terrible room. She ran as fast as she could all the way to her bedroom before slamming the door behind her and throwing herself on the bed. Tears stung her eyes as she buried her head in the blankets.

She was overwhelmed with fear and guilt, but no one was there to comfort her. She was just as alone as she had been the day she collapsed in the woods. No one cared about her, but then again, why should they after what she had just done to Master Marlow? Alvera was beating herself up over her terrible mistake.

Her conscience sounded like a crowd of people shouting at her inside her head. All that really could be heard over the deafening roars, however, was the muffled sobbing of the miserable girl. Soon the soft whimpers faded away as Alvera cried herself to sleep, but the clamorous yells persisted into her torturous dreams.

CHAPTER 7

It was a beautiful morning. Pale sunlight glittered through the curtains onto the wooden floors, birds chirped merrily outside the windows, and the tender flowers unfolded their petals to wave at the welcoming sun. All of nature was excited and invigorated for the day; but inside the house, it was a much different story. If there hadn't been any windows, one would have thought that it was nearly dusk. It was so dismal and gloomy inside that not even the sun could scatter the oppressive clouds of depression. And Master Marlow was in the deepest, darkest part of the storm. He had not slept at all last night. After lingering in the forbidden room for quite a while, he had retreated to his office to compose himself.

Now, he stood vaguely gazing out of the heavily curtained window of his study, but he wasn't seeing the sunshine. He was seeing the events of last night floating like terrible phantoms before his eyes. His anger at Alvera had subsided many hours ago. All the master felt now was crushing guilt. She hadn't meant to cause any harm. He shouldn't have lost his temper so quickly, but he had let his sensitive past control him.

Master Marlow sighed and closed his eyes. *Maybe I really am a monster,* he thought dismally to himself. *I certainly acted like one last night.* Opening his eyes, he looked out at the beautiful summer day for the first time. He flung open the curtains and was instantly engulfed in sparkling light. It was amazing how it seemed to perk everything up. How it could chase away the darkness of night. How it could reveal secrets previously unknown. Somehow, this light was contagious. It kindled a small flame of hope within the master's chest. He could not undo the damage of last night, but perhaps he could mend the wounds.

Emerging from his study, he walked purposefully down the hall. Stopping in front of Alvera's room, he raised a hand to knock but hesitated. He wasn't sure if he had the courage to go through with this. However, he knew that this was the only way to set things right. Bowing his head and taking a deep breath, Master Marlow rapped on the door.

"Alvera?" he softly called.

No answer. He knocked again.

"Alvera?"

Still no answer. Seeing that this was getting him

nowhere, the master slowly opened the door and tip-toed into the room.

"Alvera?"

It was exceedingly dark in the bedroom. Much darker than the girl normally liked. Master Marlow cautiously approached the bed. The blankets were wrinkled, but Alvera was not there. *Perhaps she decided to get up early this morning,* he reasoned. He hastily left the room and glanced across the hall. The bathroom door was ajar. She wasn't in there. Master Marlow galloped down the stairs, beginning to grow slightly worried.

"Alvera?" he called out as he marched down the lower hallway.

He poked his head like a bewildered gopher into each room he passed. She wasn't in the library, the operation room, or the closet. He rushed back into the den. She wasn't in any of the chairs, and she wasn't in the kitchen. She wasn't anywhere to be found! Now the master was really starting to panic. Where was Felix when he needed him? Darting through the kitchen, Master Marlow burst through the side door to the garden.

"Alvera!?" he yelled.

He was about to call her name again as he came to the end of the garden, but he abruptly stopped and stared straight ahead. Just a few feet away from the poplar tree sat Alvera on a little knoll in the grass. Her back was to the master, so she apparently hadn't heard or seen him. Master Marlow breathed a huge sigh of relief at the sight of her hunched back. She was still here, and more importantly, she was safe. However, the master's relief was short-lived as the real reason for his search returned to him. His heart felt as if it had sunk into the pit of his stomach. He wasn't quite sure how to handle this delicate situation, but he knew that the only way to rid himself of his guilt was to face the situation head-on.

With another deep breath, the master slowly approached the girl. She didn't flinch or even acknowledge him as he gingerly sat down beside her. Following her example, the master looked straight ahead. The yard was even more beautiful out here than it was from inside. The soft blades of grass shone like golden strands of grain in the sun's yellow touch. Several squirrels bounced around playfully from little tunnels that they had burrowed into the grass. Delicate little butterflies flittered about flashing their painted wings. All the trees seemed to glow like fireflies in the brilliant day. Even the serious spruces and pines in the woods had a more pleasant look to them. But this peaceful scene was not enough to calm the master's troubled spirit. He had to get things resolved. Clearing his throat, he turned his head toward Alvera. "Beautiful morning," he mumbled rather awkwardly.

Alvera nodded while keeping her head resolutely facing forward. Master Marlow's hopes were dampened.

It looked as if he would have to carry most of the conversation. He had barely started and was already struggling for words. After trying futilely to think of something else to say that might brighten the mood, he reluctantly decided to begin his apology.

He sighed, and a few strands of his raven hair fell over his troubled face. "Listen, Alvera," he began solemnly. "I'm sorry about last night. I shouldn't have yelled at you as I did. I let my emotions get the best of me. Please forgive me for my foolish actions."

Still without looking at him, Alvera nodded again. An instant wave of relief swept over Master Marlow, but for some reason, he still felt his heavy burden of guilt weighing heavily on his heart. Something was wrong. He gazed intently at Alvera. Her body language was a bit odd. She still hadn't even glanced at him, and now she was absent-mindedly plucking blades of grass from the ground and letting them fall through her fingers. Something seemed to be troubling her. Not wanting to ask her about it directly, the master took a different approach.

"So, why did you decide to come outside this morning? Enjoying the nice weather?"

Alvera looked up from the blades of grass that she had been fiddling with and stared with glossy eyes into the woods. Her mouth twitched uncontrollably as if she were trying to form an answer. Suddenly, she sprang off the ground.

Looking out the corners of her eyes at her surprised host, she quickly whispered, "I'm sorry!" and ran across the yard, burying her face in her hands.

Stunned by her curious actions, Master Marlow simply stared after her fleeing figure. Had he really caused her to be this upset? The master felt worse than he had before apologizing. What was he to do? Suddenly, a startling thought shocked his brain. Alvera was running straight toward the electric fence that surrounded the property, and she wasn't aware of it. Springing to his feet, Master Marlow chased after the hysterical girl.

"Alvera!" he shouted frantically as he struggled to catch up to her. "Stop! The electric fence!"

The girl was too distraught to hear his cries, and all the while, she was speeding closer and closer to the fence. Determined to stop her, Master Marlow surged forward with a rush of adrenaline. His thundering footsteps were pounding in his ears.

"Alvera!"

With a desperate lunge, he finally caught her by the shoulders. She struggled to break free from his grasp.

"Alvera, stop! Look."

Alvera ceased her squirming and looked up. Just feet away was the crackling electric fence. If the master had not caught her when he did, she would have been electrocuted. For a moment, Alvera simply stared at the fence with bulging eyes while breathing heavily from her frantic sprint. Without warning, she suddenly slipped out from the master's grip and collapsed in a heap of grief at his feet.

Master Marlow didn't know what to do. In all his years of being a doctor, he had never dealt with patients and their emotions. Dumbfounded and a bit frightened, all he could do was stare at the crumpled ball shaking at his feet. Alvera was sobbing uncontrollably with her breath occasionally hitching in her throat. He couldn't just let the poor thing lie there in a miserable heap all day. Gently, Master Marlow reached down and patted Alvera on the shoulder.

"There...there," he awkwardly soothed. "It's alright. Everything is going to be alright."

His attempt at comfort didn't seem to have any effect on the poor girl, so the master tried another tactic. Sliding his strong hands under her delicate arms, he lifted the girl to her feet. Tenderly caressing her around both shoulders, he slowly guided the tearful girl back to the house.

"Let's go back inside," he timidly suggested. "Please...don't cry. You're alright. You're alright."

Thankfully, Felix was still nowhere to be seen when the two entered the house. Master Marlow didn't want him to see the girl in this state. It might cause him to worry. Carefully leading Alvera up the stairs, he walked her to her room. He sat her on the bed and quietly returned to the doorway.

"Just rest now. Alright?"

The only response he got was the quiet, continual sobbing of the girl.

Closing the door with a soft click, Master Marlow slowly shuffled back down the hall to his study. Just as he was about to close himself in, Felix appeared at the top of the stairs.

"Oh! I'm sorry, Sir," he apologized. "I didn't mean to interrupt anything, but breakfast is ready. Shall I bring it up to you?"

"No, thank you, Felix," the master softly replied. "I'm not hungry."

The butler peered into his master's gaunt face. "Is everything alright, Sir?"

"Yes, Felix. Everything is fine. I just didn't sleep well last night."

Felix eyed Master Marlow suspiciously. He wasn't entirely convinced that the master was telling the whole truth, but not wanting to press the matter further, he changed the subject.

"What about the girl? Is she awake?"

"Yes."

"Shall I go fetch her to come down to breakfast?"

"No, she is not feeling well. Just leave her alone for the rest of the day. In fact, don't bother disturbing her tomorrow either."

"But she must eat," protested Felix.

"If she gets hungry enough, she will come out, but for now, let her be." With that, Master Marlow closed the study door on the bewildered gardener. Felix lingered in the hall a few seconds longer before pattering back down the stairs.

The master waited until he could no longer hear the thump of Felix's feet. As soon as their muffled noise faded away, he moved toward his desk. As he passed the window, he yanked the curtains closed that he had opened earlier that morning. The hope and cheer were gone. All that was left was misery and gloom. Master Marlow roughly plopped down in his chair and propped his elbows on the wooden desk.

Resting his forehead in the palms of his hands, he shook his head and muttered, "It's all my fault. All my fault."

CHAPTER 8

Alvera didn't come out of her room for the rest of that day or the next. On the morning of the third day, she still had not emerged. Felix was beginning to worry about her. While Master Marlow wasn't concerned, he did acknowledge that it was about time for her to come out. Surely, she had had enough time to calm down. So, upon Felix's urgent insistence, Master Marlow reluctantly decided to check on her. He knocked softly on the door. No response. Perhaps she was asleep.

As quietly as he could, he opened the slightly squeaky door, gently closed it behind him, and tiptoed toward the bed. As he had suspected, Alvera was asleep. He grimaced at the small bundle of blankets knotted on the bed. How could he go about waking her up gently? He took a step closer to the bed. The board beneath his shoe creaked loudly. Master Marlow winced at the shrill sound and held his breath as he nervously glanced at the girl's sleeping figure. She fidgeted a bit but remained undisturbed. The master exhaled slowly. He reached out to gently tap her, but just before his fingertips could brush her shoulder, the girl began to toss and turn. A pained expression filled her tightly shut eyes, furrowing eyebrows, and frowning lips. Her nostrils flared as her breathing quickened.

It looked as if she had been troubled by something even before now, for shiny trails of dried tears were drawn down her cheeks. Her legs began to squirm beneath the blankets as if she were trying to fight off something, and she began shaking her head violently from side to side. Inaudible whimpers soon grew into heart-stabbing moans. She began fighting so desperately in her sleep that her entire body began to writhe, along with her kicking legs and flailing arms. The moans grew louder and more terrible before they suddenly shifted into coherent words. Alvera repeated them over and over again. Suddenly, the words became clear to the master as they grew louder. As her desperate cry continued to gain volume, more emotion was being emphasized. In fact, she seemed to be almost on the verge of tears.

At the peak of her distressing cries and wild flailing, Alvera suddenly sat straight up in bed and shouted, "Mom!! Dad!!"

A wild look was in her gaping eyes as she darted her head this way and that around the room. She didn't

realize where she was for a moment, and she was beginning to panic.

"It's alright! It's alright!" Master Marlow reassured
the frightened girl. "It's just me."

Alvera stared at the master for a moment, still unsure of her surroundings. When her terror-filled eyes
suddenly met his, her heavy panting subsided into a silent flow of tears that cascaded over the former irides-
cent paths.

Master Marlow didn't know what to say after what
he had just seen. He was rather startled and confused
by the whole incident and didn't know what to make
of it. He still strongly believed that it was his fault that
the girl was so upset and seeing her in this tearful state
made him feel wretched and helpless. Instead of trying to soothe her further, the master resorted to the one
thing that he knew he could do to help.

Stretching out his hand to the girl as he knelt upon
the floor, he quietly asked, "May I see your arm?"

She nodded and placed her arm in the master's out-
stretched hand.

As he began unwrapping the bandages as he had
done so many times before, Alvera noticed that the
master's right hand was wrapped up in similar bandages. That was the hand he had smashed into the mirror a couple of nights before. Alvera lowered her gaze
as more tears fell. She still felt terrible about what had
happened in the forbidden room, and she hadn't had a

chance to apologize yet. But she just didn't know if she could express her guilt to the master right now. She was being overwhelmed with her own troubles.

As the master continued to unwrap the girl's arm, he couldn't help but look up at her bowed head. Tears were falling like rain now from her downcast eyes, and each glistening drop was like a dagger gouging into his heart. He couldn't take it anymore. He had to speak.

"I'm sorry that I have upset you so much. I can't stand to see how deeply I've hurt you. Some doctor I am."

Alvera shook her head and gasped for a steady breath. "It's not you," she sobbed.

Master Marlow froze in his work and looked up with wide eyes. Had he heard her correctly? Was he not the cause of all her sorrow?

"It's not?" he asked in a voice that was barely above a whisper.

Alvera shook her head again, "No."

"Then ... what has upset you so?"

Alvera kept shaking her head. She tried to steady her voice, but it was no use. "I ... guess ... I'm just a little ... homesick," she finally cried.

The master gazed intently at her golden head. He could tell that she had more to say, so he simply remained quiet and attentive while she released some of her pent-up emotions. When she was able to bring herself back under control, she continued.

"I just…don't know what I'm going to do. I don't even know if I have a home to go back to. You see, I was in a plane crash before you found me."

Master Marlow was completely engrossed in every word Alvera spoke.

"My parents and I had gone on vacation to visit some relatives in America. On our way back, the pilot announced that the plane was having engine trouble. Just as we were nearing the coast, one of the engines completely burned out. There was nothing the pilot could do. We were going to crash. He simply told everyone to get into a bracing position to prepare for impact. My parents knew that this meant that we would most likely die, and they wanted to make sure that I was safe.

"So, my dad broke the window next to our seats and told me to jump. We were close enough to the water that I would survive the fall, but I didn't want to leave my parents. I knew that I would be the only one to jump from the window because I was the only one small enough to fit through. I just couldn't leave my parents to the awful fate I knew awaited them, but they wouldn't listen to my protests. They forced me to jump. As I pushed my way out, the inside of my left arm scraped against the jagged edges of glass that were still in the window."

"Ah! That explains the pieces of glass," Master Marlow interrupted.

"After I hit the water, I swam to the surface just as

the plane crashed. It was awful! I screamed for my parents when I heard the plane hit the ground. The impact was so violent that it seemed to shake the entire earth! I couldn't stop staring at the trails of smoke and fire that blazed in the sky, but I suddenly remembered that I was floating in the ocean and bleeding profusely. I swam to the shore as quickly as I could and looked around. There wasn't anyone in sight that could help me. I was already exhausted from my swim to the shore, but I knew that I had to find someone. I was losing a lot of blood.

"I desperately plunged through the woods for hours until my strength left my legs. After that, I had to crawl. I was growing weaker by the minute and began to wonder if I was going to die. Suddenly, I came up to a hedge of bushes. There was a house just beyond them. I reached out my hand to continue toward it when I suddenly became very dizzy. Everything started to spin and grow dim until it was nothing but darkness. When I woke up, I was in a room with you and Mr. Felix."

The master simply stared at Alvera in stunned silence. He had no idea that she had been through so much! No wonder she was upset! As he thought on these things, a new emotion flooded his mind. Admiration. To have survived a plane crash, lost her parents, found herself in the arms of strangers, endured the master's foul temper…she must have been very brave indeed. If only he had known, he may have treated her with more kindness and understanding. But it didn't matter now. All that mattered was what he could do for the girl from here forward.

Suddenly, a new spring of tears rose to Alvera's eyes. She tried to choke them back, but they forced their way out. Master Marlow looked at her with concern.

"I'm sorry," she peeped, trying to wipe her glossy eyes. "I'm just…really scared. I don't even know if my parents are alive or not! If they are, I don't even know where to begin looking for them! And if they're not…oh! I don't mean to be ungrateful! You've done so much for me! And, I'm sorry for going into the room! I…"

Startled by a gentle touch beneath her chin, Alvera abruptly stopped in her rambling confession. Slowly, the hand under her chin raised her head until her watery eyes met Master Marlow's. He brushed some of her dangling hairs aside so that he could see her face fully.

Alvera was scared and ashamed, yet she couldn't force herself to move from his gaze. It was as if some invisible force were holding her there. Her wet cheeks began to glow with a stinging blush.

"Don't be ashamed," he hummed softly in his rumbling voice. "It's alright to cry. You've been so brave through everything you have faced, and now, you are safe. I promise to do everything I can to find your parents, but right now, it's time to let your fear go."

Alvera stared in amazement at the master. He was still the same man that she had met the day of the plane crash, but something was different about him. His combed black hair still perfectly framed his pale face. He still bore the scars and deformities of his youth, and that boil of a mole still stared at her from his bulky chin. But, the lines in his gaunt face did not seem to cut so deeply. His brows were not entwined in a stern knit. There was still a certain brevity about him, but his smiling lips betrayed other emotions. Happiness. Peace. Gentleness. Care. Things that Alvera had only caught glimpses of before now stared her fully in the face.

And for the first time, she was not afraid to look into his eyes! What used to be two pools of hatred that bored into her soul were now transformed into soft centers of black silk that sparkled gleefully whenever they saw her. Alvera beheld the same handsome face free of blemishes that she had seen the first time she was in this bedroom. But she wasn't looking out of cautious curiosity;

she was looking out of love. What she had been searching for from the master all this time had been there all along. It just needed a chance to be freed. Alvera didn't try to hold back her flood of tears any longer. She let them spill forth freely, relieved that the master finally understood and would truly be there for her whenever she needed him. Both had been freed from their cumbersome burdens.

As the last of her bitter tears fell, the master tenderly wiped her eyes. "Now, why don't we head on out? You need to get out of this room."

Master Marlow headed toward the door, but Alvera remained sitting on the bed in her bundle of blankets. She was reluctant to go. She wasn't quite sure if she had gotten over all her grief yet.

"Come," he insisted. "It does no good to sit and mourn. I know. Trust me. You'll feel much better. Besides, it looks like your arm has healed up nicely. It's time to remove the stitches."

Alvera looked up at the master and pondered on what he had said for a moment. He was right. It would be good to get out of this room for a while. Unwinding herself from the blankets and sliding off the edge of her bed, she slowly approached him. When she reached his side, Master Marlow held out his good hand to the girl. She timidly placed her small hand in his, and the two walked silently down the hall together.

CHAPTER 9

Even though a great burden had been taken away, Alvera still felt miserable. Homesickness was difficult for her to overcome. She often wandered off to a secluded corner to ruminate on her sorrows alone. Even though she knew that Master Marlow understood her pain, she still felt more comfortable expressing it away from him. She knew how intensely her tears and anguish burned his tender heart.

Indeed, the master could think of little else besides Alvera's misery. She had been such a joy to him through his own struggles, and now that her contagious happiness had seemed to vanish, his troubles were compounded. All he wanted was to bring the cheerful, complacent little girl back to him, but he wasn't quite sure how to do that. It seemed as if the only thing that would cheer her up would be the miraculous appearance of her parents. Her parents. That was another problem. Master Marlow had promised to do everything he could to find them, but he didn't even know where to begin looking. All he knew was that they had been in a plane crash just off the coast. A potentially lethal plane crash. If he were to find out that the girl's parents had indeed died, the master didn't know if he could even relate that horrible news to the already-heartbroken girl. He needed to keep a positive outlook. Perhaps they had survived along with their daughter. But again, the same question. Where was the master even to begin looking for them?

He could always send Felix inquiring at the nearest hospital, but there was no guarantee that the staff would release any information concerning the couple. In most medical practices, patient information is strictly confidential to those that are not members of the immediate family. Alvera could accompany Felix. No. She had been through too much already. There's no telling what kind of answer she would get. Furthermore, if the hospital were to find out about her involvement in the plane crash, they would question as to what happened to her and how she had survived. That probing would lead directly back to the master himself, and he certainly didn't want any public exposure. Alvera accepted him, but that didn't mean that the rest of the world would. No, he needed to stay as far away from the case as possible.

If he was going to be able to help, he would have to rely on Felix in a more local scene. It was getting close to time for Felix to head out to the market for more food and supplies. When he did go, Master Marlow would give him instructions to find out anything and everything he could about the recent plane crash. Gossip blazed like a bonfire in the little English village, and it typically burned within the neighborhood for many weeks after its first ignition. If they were going to have any chance of procuring some information concerning Alvera's parents and the crash, it would be in the village.

In the meantime, he tried to comfort Alvera in the only ways he knew how: the ways that he had used to cope with sorrow for many, many years. Ever since the day she had broken down in the front yard, Master Marlow had been busily sewing something for her. The day after their chat in the bedroom, it was ready. That afternoon, the master found Alvera back outside on the little mound in the yard. She was hunched over in a depressed slouch staring aimlessly at the ground. The blades of grass blurred before her almost in a dream-like haze as tears slowly pooled in her eyes. She knew that she mustn't dwell on the horrific crash that still seemed as if it had happened only minutes ago, but she just didn't know how to distract herself from it.

How had she been able to do so all the time that she had been here? Perhaps she had been so distracted with the unfamiliarity of the place and of the people that she had forgotten to be upset. If only she could forget again. But as soon as she thought about the peace of forgetfulness, she was instantly driven to guilt. She couldn't just forget about her parents like that! What if they were still alive? What if they were injured and nobody knew where they were? What if they were earnestly searching for their lost daughter? The welling tears began to drop.

As Alvera continued to silently battle with her emotions, Master Marlow slowly approached from behind. He stopped a little distance away, careful not to let his elongated shadow fall in front of her. Bending down, he gently draped his handywork around her sagging shoulders. Alvera jumped when she felt the fabric brush her arms. Looking down, she watched as the master carefully tied two silk ribbons into a bow around her neck. When he was done, she looked around at the beautiful powder-blue cloak that swaddled her before turning to look up at the master. He wore a grave expression.

"It will help."

Before she could utter a thank you, Master Marlow nodded and walked silently back to the house.

To her surprise, the new cloak did help to ease some of her sadness. Whenever she felt like crying, she simply wrapped the blue folds tightly around herself like a blanket. It felt as if someone were giving her a comforting hug. She could see why Master Marlow always wore his cloak. It seemed to hide what one was feeling inside while helping to cope with the issues at the same time. But Alvera knew that the cloak wasn't the answer to her problems. It was simply there for comfort. In fact, it wasn't even the cloak that gave her the most comfort; it was the master's kindness. He cared for her so much that he took the time to make something special to help her.

A new love was beginning to grow inside Alvera. Master Marlow felt like another father to her. She felt safe and secure whenever he was around, and that was a feeling that she had never felt so completely with anyone other than her real mother and father. And little did he realize, but that same love was beginning to bud within Master Marlow as well. Alvera wasn't just a special little girl that understood him like no one else ever had; she was family. She was like the daughter he never had. Soon, he would understand just what that meant to him.

By that evening, Alvera was feeling a little better and was able to coax Master Marlow outside. The sun had just set when the two ventured out. A balmy night was dawning over the tips of the trees, and this sultry haze flushed the fireflies out from the bushes. The luminous beetles flashed their yellow and green lanterns as they floated through the muggy air. Alvera felt as if she were walking in the midst of twinkling Christmas lights hovering in the night. There was something magical about it all.

Suddenly, she pointed excitedly toward a firefly flashing nearby. The master chuckled to himself as he watched the girl rush over to the fleeting light. Seconds later, she was running back to him with tightly cupped hands. She smiled eagerly at the master and held her cupped hands up to him. As she slowly opened them, Master Marlow saw a flicker of light as a tiny firefly flew up into the sky. The little insect twinkled alongside the millions of stars that speckled the night. Both gazed in amazement until the firefly had flown so high that he could not be distinguished from the stars. Alvera's spirits seemed to lift with the luminescent beetle. With a cheerful laugh, she twirled off to join the rest of the fireflies in their dance.

Master Marlow's grin widened as he watched her dance lightly on her feet as if she didn't have a care in the world. His eyelids halfway closed lazily in content-ment as his mind began to wander in the trance of the fireflies.

This is what he had hoped for. Alvera was more herself tonight. Out playing with the creatures she so dearly loved. It was good for her to have time to release her grief, but now it was time to move past it. The master would need to keep her mind occupied. Tonight was a great start; however, he would also need to constantly encourage her. Her confidence was extremely fragile, and worrying about her parents had only made it weaker. He would need to keep her hopes up, but not too much.

If it turned out that her parents were dead, the master wouldn't want her spirit to be destroyed by the news. So just to be safe, Master Marlow wouldn't tell Alvera about Felix's mission that he had planned. It all depended on what Felix would discover in the village as to what the master would do or say. It was a very delicate matter. Suddenly, a thought crossed his mind that he had not considered before. If they learned that the girl's parents were alive and were able to locate them, what would happen then? Obviously, the girl would return home with her parents, but what would become of Master Marlow? The thought troubled him greatly. He hadn't considered what would happen once Alvera was gone.

In fact, he had become so accustomed to her presence that the master had forgotten that her departure was going to be real. He could not bear to think about it. Why did it bother him so? Returning the girl to her parents. This was his goal. Wasn't it?

The night seemed much darker when Master Marlow awoke from his reverie. He looked around in surprise. Not a single firefly was to be found, and only moments before, the air had been swarming with them! Through the shadowy gloom, he spotted Alvera standing several feet away. A mischievous smirk graced her lips and glittered in her eyes. The master gave her a perplexed look as he studied her more closely. There was something odd about the way she was holding her cloak. Suddenly, she flung open the pale fabric. As soon as she did, hundreds of fireflies scattered into the air. Somehow, she had managed to capture all of them while Master Marlow had been pondering! The master's jaw dropped in bewildered surprise as his eyes darted from one firefly to the other that hummed by his ears. Alvera couldn't contain her amusement any longer. Master Marlow jerked his head toward her as uncontrollable laughter bubbled out of her mouth. It was contagious laughter, for the master soon found himself laughing right along with her. Youthful laughter. How good it felt! It had been such a long time since he had laughed like that that he had forgotten just how warm it made him feel inside.

One seemed to forget all his worries when such joy exploded out of him. It was rejuvenating. But the joy didn't stay for long. It died away like the fading of a firefly's glow and was replaced with cold sorrow. It was moments like these that reminded Master Marlow not to take happiness for granted. It visited him rarely in times of stress. There were serious things to be taken care of, and one of those things had been constantly nagging at him for several days. It was time to deal with it. He could not avoid it any longer.

* * *

Early the next morning before the sun peeked its sleepy head over the horizon, Master Marlow gently woke Alvera and quietly led her down the hall. He wanted to execute his plan while Felix was still asleep. Stopping in front of the forbidden room, he hurriedly jerked out a key from the depths of his cloak and jammed it into the keyhole. As soon as the door unlocked with a surprisingly loud click, he swiftly stalked inside. He assumed that Alvera had followed obediently behind him, but as he approached the wall of mirrors, he saw her reflection still timidly standing outside the open door. She was hesitant to enter, and he understood why. The last time she had been in this room, she had been shouted at by the master himself. She didn't want to push her boundaries again. But this time, it was different. Master Marlow turned toward the frightened girl and gently reassured her. "Come. It's alright."

Still bearing the signs of trepidation, Alvera warily tiptoed over the threshold and slowly advanced a little way into the room.

"Close the door, if you would."

Alvera obeyed but remained standing at the door. She was extremely uncomfortable and wanted to bolt. Master Marlow could read these feelings in her frightened eyes. He was going to show her that she had no need to be afraid. "Come here."

He waited until Alvera had joined him by his side before he continued in subdued tones.

"The last time you were in this room, I didn't exactly give you a very good explanation concerning the various items you see here. I can't hide it from you any longer. You deserve to know. After all, you shared your story with me; it is only fair that I now share mine. I want to share it. There is no need to be afraid."

Upon hearing those last words, she relaxed a bit. His attitude was much different than last time. In fact, he had even invited her in here! Perhaps there was nothing to fear. After all, Master Marlow was here to help her. She could trust him.

"Let's begin over here," he said as he led her over to the two walls that were covered in a collage of pictures.

"These are portraits of my family. Many of them came from my mother's house where I grew up. You see this picture?" he asked as he pointed to the young black-haired boy in the small oval frame. "You've probably already figured it out by now, but that was me as a boy. Why do I look so sad? Why does everyone look sad for that matter? Well, to understand that, I must start from the beginning.

"My mother had already given birth to a baby boy two years before I was born. When the family found out that she was pregnant again, they were so excited. That would be the last and only time they would ever be excited about me. After I was born, my family was horrified. I was perfectly healthy, but I had been born with deformed ears and a small lump on my back. The doctors informed my parents that this lump was the beginning of a stooped posture. As I grew older, the lump would gradually worsen until I became a hunchback. They said that I would never have straight posture. My family didn't understand. What had my parents done wrong to produce such a malformed child? You see, my family prided itself in perfection.

"Up until my birth, not a single child had been born with any blemishes or deformities. To them, I was a disappointment. They were ashamed to admit they were related to me. I was the reject, and that's the way they treated me. Even my own father despised me. But in the face of all the opposition, there was one who cared for me. My mother. She was never very open with me or expressive with her emotions, but I could sense that she was the one person who would be there for me.

"A year later, my younger brother, Michael, was born. Just like my older brother, Andrew, Michael was 'perfect.' Things only worsened from there. Not only was I the cursed child of the family, but now I was also the middle child. I rarely received any attention, especially while Michael was a baby. My mother had to care for all three of us herself because my father worked during the day. Even when he arrived home in the evenings, my mother was still left to take care of all the housework. But despite how exhausted she was, my mother always took the time to pull me onto her skinny knee and give me a hug before she laid me down for bed.

"In my early years, I tried to gain attention from my father. I would waddle up to his massive armchair and hold my tiny arms up for him to lift me off the ground, but I was always met with a snarling grimace from behind a newspaper. I quickly learned to avoid him. He didn't care about me. As my brothers and I grew, they didn't seem to care about me either. Andrew would only play with Michael. When I would try to join them, he often pushed me away. Sometimes he would shove me so forcefully that I would fall completely onto my back and knock my head against the wooden floors. My father always laughed.

"Despite how cruel Andrew was to me, Michael wasn't any kinder. As soon as he learned how to make faces, Michael started copying my father's grimace whenever I passed by. So, I often wandered off on my own to play. My only friends were rocks, twigs, and frogs that I found outside. They didn't make good conversation, but at least they didn't hate me.

"When my fifth birthday came, I was so excited. I would finally be attending school. I was excited because I had always loved learning new things, but most of my excitement was over the fact that for several hours each day, I would be away from my family. No glaring, no shoving, and no yelling. Just school and possibly friends that wouldn't judge me. However, these hopes were soon dashed into a million broken pieces.

"A few days after I had turned five years old, my brothers and I were playing outside. I was off on my own as usual. That day, I had wandered closer to the woods surrounding our house than ever before. As I squatted down to poke at the dirt with a stick, I heard a rustle in the low brambles of the woods. When I looked up to see what it was, a hungry wolf lunged out of the shadows and clobbered me with his massive body. There wasn't anything I could do except scream and cry out for help. My parents eventually came charging out of the house and scared the wolf away, but by that time, I had sustained serious wounds. I was covered in blood from head to toe. The wolf had bitten and clawed all over my body. In some places, particularly on my back, huge chunks of flesh had been completely ripped out by his powerful jaws. For the rest of my life, I would bear the ugly scars that the wolf gave me, and those scars would only cause more misfortune.

"It took an exceedingly long time for my wounds to mend enough for me to be able to move about again. Because of this, I wasn't able to start school until late in the winter. It was bad enough having to catch up on the material that the other children had already learned; what was even worse was facing the other children themselves. From the moment I walked into that class-room, every eye was glued to me. Everyone constantly stared at the stitches zigzagging across my face. The one thing I couldn't hide. Huddled groups would whisper to each other whenever I passed by in the halls, and the shocked stares soon turned into disgusted glances. None of the other students ever spoke to me unless it was to poke fun. I had no hope of making any friends at school. I couldn't trust anyone.

"The loneliness and bullying I faced in school only progressed as I got older. In seventh grade, the bullying reached its climax. As I was hurrying down the hall to one of my classes, one of my toughest bullies blocked my path. He spat out a few jeering remarks. I ignored him and replied that I needed to get to class. A look of pure loathing enflamed his face before he punched me right in the nose. I felt the bone collapse with an earsplitting crunch as soon as he hit me. When we went to the doctor, I found out that my nose had been completely shattered. The doctor wrapped it up as best he could, but the bones never grew back straight. I would have a crooked nose for the rest of my life. I had already been teased enough over the years about my large proboscis. Its crooked lump only made it more of a target.

"After I graduated high school, a small flower of hope began to grow inside me. I was moving on to college. Since those students would be more mature, perhaps I would finally be released from my torture of bullying. How wrong I was. Everyone had been cordial on the first day of introductions, but once classes began, the joking never ceased. From that moment on, I never attempted to form friendships. I isolated myself from every other student and completely engrossed myself in my studies. The only people I did talk to were my professors. After all, they were the only ones who seemed to care or show any interest in me. I eventually convinced myself that I didn't have time for friends. My goal to become a doctor was much more important to me.

"I had always had a fascination with living things, and I had always loved anatomy. But perhaps the biggest reason why I chose to become a doctor was because of what had happened to me. I had this desire to help others that had been injured, even though they didn't care about me. Even if it were my greatest enemy, I would never want him to experience the pain that I had known. Perhaps that was my way of reaching out to a world that I could never hope to join.

"Upon graduation, I immediately set out to look for openings in different doctors' offices. It wasn't long before I found a place in need of a physician's assistant. I applied and got the job. To be an assistant wasn't my dream job, but it was a great place to start and build up my experience. It had only been a week when the doctor called me in to his office to talk. He seemed quite sincere when he told me how impressed he was with my skills in the medical field, but despite his delight in having me and training me, he told me that I could not remain there. Several complaints had come in regarding my frightful appearance. Apparently, some patients felt so uncomfortable around me that they were considering changing doctors. The doctor hated to send me away, but he couldn't afford to lose business. The office had few patients as it was. Heartbroken, I left.

"My curse had followed me into my career. But I wasn't about to give up. A week later, I found another office looking for a male nurse. The staff eagerly hired me, but this time, I only lasted three days before they kicked me out for the same reason as the office I had worked at before. I quickly found another office in need of more workers, but I was turned away as soon as they saw me. Obviously, they knew I was a hindrance before they even gave me a chance. After three failed attempts at keeping a job, I was ready to give up. The same thing was just going to keep happening no matter where I went; however, I couldn't help scanning the windows of offices and clinics for job opportunities even as I moped along the streets.

"On one of those occasions, I passed by a clinic that had an opening for a doctor. I couldn't believe my eyes. My dream job was plastered against those front windows. I had no idea if I even had a shot of getting the position, but I dashed inside that building anyway. The staff was exuberant. No one had applied for the job in nearly a month, and the second doctor was struggling to attend to all the retired doctor's patients. I was their new doctor.

"For a while, everything was wonderful. I was finally able to grasp the dream that had seemed so far away just a few weeks before. There was this joy that filled my heart every time I sewed a stitch or bandaged a wound. It was my passion to help people, and during that time, I was the happiest that I had been in many, many years. But the happiness soon faltered. Only a few months into my new position, I started to notice that I couldn't keep the same patients. The list of names constantly changed, which was difficult because I had to adjust to each new patient's anatomy. Soon, the list began to shrink until I had no more patients.

"I sat for one week in my office without having to see anybody. It was depressing. The other doctor in the office noticed this and tried to transfer some of his patients over to me. Most people refused, and many others were outraged. The situation was becoming very intense, and I didn't want anyone else to suffer because of me. To protect the business and the staff, I reluctantly resigned from my position as doctor. This was the toughest decision I ever made. It broke my heart to leave what I enjoyed so much, but I moved forward with a new ambition. As much as I enjoyed helping the sick, my real passion was centered on helping the injured. If I couldn't be a doctor, perhaps I could become a surgeon.

"I went back to school and earned my master's in advanced surgery. I was now an expert surgeon looking for a job. Instead of meeting an employer in person this time, I decided to send my application by mail. Almost all the clinics and hospitals that I sent my application to offered me a job. At first, I wasn't sure which one to choose, but I eventually decided to help the place that needed it the most. My first week there, I only had one surgery to perform. I worried that this job was going to abandon me just like all the others had. Business for me was slow for a while, but pretty soon, patients were coming in for surgery every day of the week. I didn't want to get too confident, but it seemed as if I was there for good. After a year at the clinic, patients started requesting me specifically for surgery. They were so impressed with my work that they even referred me to others they knew. It seemed as if overnight I had become the most popular person in the medical field. I was stunned. No one, besides my mother, had ever valued me until now.

"My dream had expanded into something bigger than I had ever imagined. I had been accepted by the world around me. It was a wonderful feeling. Almost as wonderful as the joy I received from helping others. But I had to remind myself that the world only loved what I did. They did not love me, and I never gave them a chance to. From the moment I became a surgeon, I insisted that the patients be sedated before coming back to me. If they should ever see who their surgeon was, I feared that my career would end, along with my joy. I couldn't bear to feel that cold rejection again. I had to keep this job. I just had to.

"For several years, I worked in this way of secrecy and was extremely successful. I was even voted the best surgeon in the entire country. People from every corner of England and beyond flocked to my office. But I didn't want any of the attention or praise that I received; I just wanted to quietly help others as I had always done. Several patients wanted to meet me so that they could thank me in person, but I always refused. They could not meet me. I would not let them. It would destroy me, and several of my colleagues knew this. Four of my assistants in the operating room had been trying for positions as professional surgeons for years without success. They envied me greatly and despised my abilities. I was known for attention to detail, precise incisions, careful stitching, meticulous work, and gentle care with my patients. In all my years as a surgeon, not one of my surgeries had gone wrong. My assistants had always been there to ensure a perfect procedure for each patient. This time, however, was different.

"While I was preparing to perform gallbladder surgery on a patient, my assistants gathered the equipment that I would need. Little did I know that they had rubbed a dangerous bacterium all over my incision utensils. With my knowing assistants at my side, I performed the surgery. Everything went well. A few days after the surgery, however, my patient developed a serious infection that was beginning to spread from her incision site into the rest of her abdomen. I was horrified.

Nothing like this had ever happened before. I didn't understand it, but I naturally blamed myself for the accident. Thankfully, the other physicians at the clinic were
able to stop the infection before it spread any further,
and the woman recovered. The night the other doctors
informed me that the woman would be alright, I went
home feeling depressed and extremely guilty. I had always practiced careful methods and kept a steady hand.
What could have gone wrong?

"When I arrived back at the clinic the next morning, I was met with a newspaper stapled to the cork board outside my office. I nearly fainted at the sight of it. On the front page was an article about my recent surgery mishap. It was entitled, 'Frankenstein is Your Doctor.' The title portrayed me as a monster, but that wasn't the worst of it. Covering half the page above the article was an exaggerated picture of my face. My scars had been darkened, my eyes had been given the blank stare of a zombie, more lines had been etched into my face, and my crooked nose had been enlarged—as if it needed that—to make me look like some gruesome menace to society.

"My heart was pounding and what color I had in my skin drained away as a cold, clammy sweat broke out all over my body. The first thought that ran through my head was, 'How had anyone obtained a picture of me?' The only picture I had of myself at the office was the picture on my identification card which I kept locked in a drawer in my office. The next thought that occurred to me was, 'Who could have done this?' Obviously, it had to have been someone who worked in the clinic. No one else would have access to my office. As my mind raced in alarming confusion, a sudden sorrow crept over me. It didn't really matter who had done this or how they had managed to do it. My face was exposed to the world. It was all over.

"A few days after the release of the article, several of

my patients cancelled their surgeries. I was so dejected. I felt like a failure and began to doubt my abilities. To make matters worse, the lady that had been the victim of the unfortunate surgery brought a lawsuit against the clinic. People began to question me, and I continued to lose more and more patients. No one trusted me anymore. They accused me of not practicing adequate sanitation before surgery. I was being attacked from all sides: the news, the press, my patients, and my fellow staff members. Soon, my surgeries stopped all together. My perfect world had crashed on top of me, breaking me into a million pieces along with it. How would I ever recover from this?

"As I sat in my office one day brooding over my ruined career, my assistants walked by. One of them patted me on the shoulder and said, 'Cheer up, Mal. Everyone makes mistakes every now and then.' Another one of them called from the hall, 'Yeah. Just remember. Next time, ya might want to clean your instruments. That is … if there is a next time!' All of them went cackling down the hall. As soon as the one assistant in the hall had said those words, I knew what had happened. They had infected my utensils … on purpose! I knew that my assistants had always been jealous of me and my position, but I never thought that they would go so far as to endanger a patient's life. And now, they were blaming me for it.

"It was too late to reveal the truth. The damage had

already been done. Besides, I had no evidence to convict my assistants of what they had done. It was my word against theirs. A combination of outrage and hurt welled up inside of me. If they wanted the job that badly, they could have it. I wasn't going to put up with this any longer. In a moment of pure rashness, I packed up all my books, documents, identification, utensils, and medicine into my leather suitcase and marched out of that clinic without so much as an explanation to my actions. I never looked back. I was done. Done with the world. It didn't appreciate me. Too many people had wounded me too deeply, and by violating my most sensitive policy, they had gone too far.

"Well, they were certain never to see any more of me. I was going to hide myself from the world's prying eyes once and for all. To do this, I went to a secluded, coastal village that my family and I used to visit occasionally when I was a boy. I bought a house there and began fortifying it against the world. I also made a cloak to conceal myself. There would inevitably be times when I would have to venture out to the village to buy necessities for myself. When those times came, I wanted protection from the people there.

"So, I've lived a recluse life in this house ever since. You already know all about Felix, but when I rescued him, he relieved me of the burdensome duty of travelling to the village. He also allowed me to vanish from society even more. No one knows that I even exist. They all think that this is Felix's house." He sighed. "But it is better like this. To shut out the world. Of course, that world found me again when you entered mine."

Master Marlow attempted a feeble smile at Alvera. She simply stared back with pity and sympathy.

"But you are not like everyone else," he continued. "You are kind and understanding. I can trust you. It's the rest of the world that I cannot trust. Or…at least…it is that way now."

The master solemnly walked over to the chests on the opposite side of the room and opened one. Inside was a mess of papers that looked as if they had just been thrown haphazardly in. He grabbed one of the topmost papers.

"Here," he said as he handed it to Alvera. "It's the article, if you'd like to see it."

She gently took the old article from him and began scanning the columns. Master Marlow folded his hands behind him and stalked over to the wall of mirrors while she read.

"As soon as I graduated high school," he mused aloud more to himself than to Alvera, "I packed up my things and left home. I couldn't wait to be out of that house, and my father and brothers were eager to see me go. I didn't say goodbye or tell my family where I was going. I just left. My mother ran out onto the front porch after me and called my name, but I ignored her tearful cries and kept going. I regret my actions now. She was the one person in my life that had cared about me. The one person I could always count on to be there for me. I don't know if she ever loved me, but…I certainly didn't show her any love that day. After everything she had done for me…that was my final action toward her. I know I broke her heart, but there is no mending it now. I cannot go back. What happened in the past is done."

Alvera looked up from the article. Master Marlow was standing in front of the mirrors with his eyes closed and his head hanging in a most dejected manner. He was grieving inside. She knew it. Slowly, she approached his hunched figure until she was standing right beside him. The master sensed her presence and looked up slightly.

"Do you know why I have these mirrors in here?" he muttered quietly. "They remind me of how the world sees me. How hideous I am. Why I can never go back. The world only sees me as a monster. Not as one of them. And, you know…sometimes I believe them. Perhaps I really am a monster. I mean…look at me! Look at what I've done!"

Alvera looked deeply into the mirror for a moment and pondered. "You don't look like a monster to me," she suddenly responded in a meek voice. "Look." She held up the article to where the distorted picture of Master Marlow was reflected in the mirrors.

"This doesn't look like you at all. You're not cruel, unfeeling, or barbaric as this picture makes you out to be. You are kind, caring, and gentle, and all that shines through your scars. I saw it the first time I looked into your face. Don't listen to the judgement of the world. All that matters is if you're doing right, and if you are, you will truly love yourself for who you are. You're not a monster. In my opinion, I think you are very handsome."

The master was speechless. A slight blush rose to his cheeks, turning part of his scars purple as he gazed over at Alvera. Handsome? Him? Did she really just say that? Suppressing his blush, Master Marlow swallowed to clear his throat from the lump that had formed in it.

"Well, you are the first person to ever tell me that. I thank you."

Alvera smiled at the master and nodded. He had a boyish look of delight on his face, but it soon faded into concern. "I understand what you said about not letting what the world thinks bother me. You're right. It doesn't matter what other people think. But I don't understand what you mean about loving myself. How do I do that? I'm ashamed to admit it, but … I really don't know much about love."

Still smiling, Alvera took the master by the hand. "I think you do know a little bit … from your mother. But I can help you understand more … if you'll let me."

Master Marlow looked into Alvera's innocent blue eyes. All he could see was love. Then he realized, it had been there all along. He just hadn't recognized it. At that moment, the plant flourishing inside the master came into full bloom. He didn't just care deeply about the girl; he loved her. He loved her as a father loves his own daughter. But he wanted to understand this love more fully.

As a tender smile slowly crept across his glowing face, he whispered, "I will."

CHAPTER 10

"This is really starting to become a bad habit of yours, Sir," remarked Felix after he had spotted an untouched plate of food from dinner that night.

Master Marlow ignored his reprimand and continued to pace the floor of his study. He was too troubled to even think about eating. Recognizing his distress, Felix attempted to calm the master's nerves by gently talking to him as he always did. "What is troubling you this time, Sir? It seems to me that there is nothing to be concerned about. You've made a wonderful friendship with the girl. You've been there to comfort her in her times of sorrow, and now, it seems as if she has fully healed."

"But that's just the problem, Felix!" Master Marlow burst out passionately. "She *has* completely healed. There's nothing more I need to do for her."

"Ah. I see. Very well, Sir. Shall I take the girl off in the morning then?"

"No."

Felix was not surprised by his answer. He knew that the master had grown to love Alvera even though he had never wanted to admit it, but Felix wanted to challenge him. Slowly, he approached the master as he sat down in his desk chair while massaging his head. "But, Sir," he began shrewdly, "is that not what you instructed me to do?"

"It is," Master Marlow painfully muttered.

"You have carried through with your promise."

"I know."

"So, after all this time, are you really going to break the rest of it?"

"I…I don't know."

There was an awful misery in that last faltering sentence. Such a sorrow that the butler had never heard from his master before. It touched his heart. Master Marlow surely was in a heart-wrenching conflict with himself. He was warily dodging the butler's sly tactic. Softening his approach, Felix tried another way. "Oh, Sir. I can't stand to see you so torn up over this. If it's bothering you this much, why don't you just forget about your promise? I'll figure something out."

"No, no," the master moaned. "I can't forget. But I can't continue either. I…I just don't know what to do."

"You could always invite the girl to stay."

Master Marlow shot Felix a wary look. His butler was taking advantage of him in his vulnerable state.

He didn't want Felix getting any ideas about his new-found love for Alvera. He had to play this very carefully. "What makes you think that I would do that?" he softly asked.

"Well, you have been spending a lot of time with the girl lately, Sir. I just figured…perhaps…there was some connection…you know…to your distress. That's all."

"Figuring always gets you into trouble, Felix. I don't appreciate your suppositions."

"It was purely a suggestion, Sir. Purely a suggestion. I'm not going to force you to do anything that makes you feel uncomfortable."

"I know."

Master Marlow gave a wide yawn which infected Felix. "Let me rest now, Felix. It's been a draining day. And you deserve a good night's sleep as well. You look quite exhausted."

"Yes, Sir. Thank you, Sir. Shall I take your plate?"

"Just leave it."

Felix nodded and slipped through the door. Before heading down the hall to his room, however, he turned back to look at the master. "Aren't you going to bed, Sir?"

"No, not yet. But don't wait up for me, Felix. I'm just going to think things over in here for a little while longer."

"Alright. Goodnight, Sir."

"Goodnight, Felix."

With that, Felix quietly shut the door and thumped his way down the hall. Master Marlow leaned over his desk as he listened to the muffled click of Felix's bedroom door echo through the hall. There was nothing for the master to consider. His mind was already made up. He just didn't know how he was going to explain his decision to Alvera. As he sat there pondering, his eyelids grew exceedingly heavy. The dim room began shifting in and out of focus. He tried to keep his mind clear enough to think, but he just couldn't fight off the urge to sleep. Without warning, his weary head dropped onto his desk with a slight thud. It had been a long time since the master had gotten a good rest, but tonight, he relaxed peacefully in a deep, dreamless sleep.

It was 8:30 in the morning when Felix realized that the master still wasn't up. It was exceedingly unusual. Felix checked the master's bedroom first, but he wasn't in there. Next, he headed to the study. Peeking his head around the door, he spotted the master flopped over on his desk asleep. The butler chuckled to himself as he crossed the room to his sleeping master's side. He gently shook Master Marlow's arm.

"Good morning, Sir. Time to wake up."

Master Marlow snorted and woke with a start. Slowly, he lifted his heavy head and looked around the room in bewilderment.

"You fell asleep in your study last night, Sir," Felix

explained to the dazed doctor. "But I'm happy to see that you got a very good night's sleep. Now, come along downstairs. Breakfast is ready."

With his body and mind finally starting to shake off his sleep, Master Marlow remembered his thoughts from last night. "Where's Alvera?" he asked in a more conscious voice.

"Oh, she's outside up that tree again. I just called her in for breakfast though, so she should be along any minute now."

"Hold off on breakfast for a moment, Felix," Master Marlow hurriedly directed as he sprang from his chair to the door with a sudden burst of energy. "Why don't you go make the beds instead? I'll just be a minute."

The confused and disgruntled butler replied, "But… I've already made the beds, Sir."

"Well, how about…opening the windows?"

"I've already done that too, Sir. And washed the laundry, cleaned the kitchen, pruned the garden, washed off my shoes…"

"What have you not done yet?" interrupted Master Marlow rather impatiently.

"I haven't refilled the oil lamps yet or…"

"Good. You do that, Felix."

The baffled butler tried to stutter something in protest, but the master had already sprinted down the stairs before he could get the words out.

Master Marlow didn't stop running until he reached

the tall poplar tree outside. He got there just in time, for Alvera was almost at the bottom.

"Alvera!" he cried rather loudly as she was placing her foot on a lower branch.

The sudden yell frightened her and caused her foot to slip. She was left dangling from the branch that her hands had been firmly latched to. She looked down. It wasn't that far of a jump. Master Marlow rushed to help her down, but before he could grab her, Alvera released her grip on the branch and dropped to the ground. Upon landing, she lost her balance and fell backwards with a small thud. The master leaned over her and gently pulled her up by the hand.

"I'm so sorry," he apologized. "I really do have bad timing whenever I come looking for you."

"Oh, no! You're fine," Alvera reassured him as she dusted herself off.

Master Marlow scolded himself on the inside. What a great way to start this whole thing off. Well, at least Alvera was an extremely easy-going child.

Several awkward minutes of silence passed as the master tried to think of how to approach the conversation. Finally, he simply gave up and reverted to his typical escape route.

"May I see your arm?"

Alvera nodded and extended it out to him. He did not have to unwrap her arm as he had in the past, for her stitches had been gone for quite some time. He simply examined the pearly scar. Everything looked completely normal, but he had already known that. He was simply looking to give himself more time to think. Slowly, his eyes wandered from the girl's arm up to her face. He lowered her arm and turned away before he became lost in her crystal blue eyes. "Well, it looks as though you're all healed up," he mumbled gravely as he rose from kneeling in the moss.

Alvera detected his dismay at her recovery and was confused. Something was wrong. She watched with deep concern as Master Marlow walked around to the trunk of the poplar and sat down on its mossy bed. Quietly, she settled herself beside him. She had this feeling that he needed company right then.

Neither of them spoke for the longest time. They simply sat in silence together, gazing at the fresh summer morning. Unexpectedly, Master Marlow broke the silence with a low whisper.

"I just feel terrible. I tried to help, but...in the end...I only made things worse. No matter what I do, this curse infects it. Please forgive me. My curse has now spread to you."

Alvera looked down at her scarred arm and back at Master Marlow. This wasn't his fault. He needed to know that once and for all. "Mr. Marlow," she quietly spoke, "you are not cursed. The scars and deformities you bear are not contagious. They are a part of you. They are a part of life. Look."

She uncovered the back of her left knee. In the bend of it was a dark purple scar.

"This is just one scar I have. Another is on my back, and another is on my head. I have had stitches before. This isn't the first time. I know what it is like to live with scars. It's nothing to be ashamed of. You see? I'm not so different from you."

The master was surprised by how many scars the girl already had at such a young age, but then again, he had sustained his at a young age as well. Slowly, he unbuttoned his right sleeve and rolled it up to reveal part of his right arm. Hundreds of shimmering lines were slashed across his flesh in all directions. Alvera could imagine just how mangled his arm must have been when those wounds had been fresh.

"You see these slashes? I cover myself for a reason. My entire body looks as if it had been fed through a shredder. I cannot let the world see these hideous marks. How could I not be ashamed?"

"Do you remember what I said yesterday? It doesn't matter what the world thinks. What matters is if you love yourself for who you are. In order to love yourself, you must appreciate the way God made you. Do you?"

"Well," Master Marlow thought, "I do like being a doctor. I feel like I'm able to do something good for others. But there are some things I'd like to change about my appearance. I don't mind my big nose or chin so much, but I definitely would like to have normal ears, a straight back, no scars, and this mole … this mole has to go!"

Alvera giggled at the master's last comment, but she quickly regained her serious composure. "That's a good start. God gave you your excellent skills as a doctor, and it's wonderful that you want to use them to help others. However, you also have to love the physical way God made you. It's wishful thinking to change all those things you mentioned about yourself, and that's really all they are. Wishes. The reality is that you do have all those blemishes. You have to look past them into here."

Leaning over, Alvera gently pressed her small hand

against Master Marlow's chest. He looked at her hand and then at her. Alvera's sweet face was radiating with love as it had been the other day. Her blue eyes were positively glowing with joy. A soft smile rested on her youthful face. The master smiled as he finally understood. Love could take many different forms, but for him to love himself, he had to stop looking at all the things he didn't love and focus on the good things inside him. Alvera was right, as usual. This is the way God had made him, and if God loved him the way he was, why shouldn't he do the same?

Alvera pulled her hand away but continued looking at Master Marlow. "That's how you love yourself," she whispered.

Reaching his arm around her narrow shoulders, Master Marlow pulled Alvera into his embrace. "Thank you, Alvera. Thank you."

Slowly, he retracted his arm. He felt that now he was ready to tell her what he had originally come to discuss. "Alvera?"

"Yes?"

"I didn't just come out here to talk to you about how well your arm has healed. There is something else I need to tell you. The night I brought you into my house, I made a vow. I vowed to care for you until you were well. As soon as that day came, I wanted Felix to take you away to wherever you needed to go because I was ready to be rid of you. Well, that day has come. But I am not the same man that I was that night. You have been a joy to me, Alvera. I never thought it would happen, but…you have changed the way I see things. As a new man, I would now like to change my vow. Even though you are well now, you may stay here with Felix and me until we find your parents. I want you to stay."

The brightest smile that the master had ever seen was spread across Alvera's face. A wave of gratitude washed over him. He was relieved that she was not hurt by his original feelings toward her. She understood why that was, and it didn't matter now. Nodding her head in appreciation, she quietly breathed, "Thank you."

Both Master Marlow and Alvera jumped when a sharp clapping sound rang out from the side door of the house. Turning toward the alarming sound, both saw that Felix was standing in the doorway applauding. Suddenly, he bounded like a bunny across the yard toward them.

"Oh! Master Marlow!" he shouted excitedly in a rather high-pitched voice. "I knew it! I just knew this day would come at last! I must admit, there were times when I thought that you had clamped up for good, but once Alvera came into your life, I knew that it was only a matter of time before you opened your locked doors. Oh! This is wonderful! I'm so happy I could just…"

In the midst of a bowlegged jump, Felix suddenly froze, and his triumphant expression melted into terror. Master Marlow was giving Felix the deadliest stare that

Alvera had ever seen. His snarling lips seemed to say, "Felix, if you keep this up, I'm going to kill you!" Alvera almost thought she heard a low growl rumbling in the master's throat! Felix quickly understood his silent message and amended what he had intended to say... "I think I'll just...go back inside and reheat the tea."

The intimidated butler sprinted back to the house as fast as his quivering legs could go. For a few moments longer, the master stared after Felix to make sure he didn't try to poke his curious nose back outside. Remembering that Alvera was still with him, he softened his expression and turned back to her. She was shocked when a roar of laughter erupted from Master Marlow's mouth. It was a contagious laughter, and she soon found herself laughing right along with the jubilant doctor. She didn't understand what was so comical about the situation, but she was pleased to see Master Marlow happy once again.

CHAPTER 11

The master's happiness continued over the next few days. In fact, it seemed as if he had finally been freed from all his burdens that had chained him to his troubled past. He resumed his apprenticeship with Alvera, smiled more frequently, and even began walking through the woods with her every day. He was not letting his fears confine him within his home anymore. And yet, he was still holding himself back. As the days passed, Alvera noticed a shade of sadness that began to darken his joyful countenance once again. The master's spurts of sorrow had always concerned her, but this time, she was deeply worried. He wasn't merely bothered by something; he was depressed. And that depression's intensity increased every day. What worried her even more was the fact that the master had not yet voiced his troubles to her as he had in the past. Perhaps he thought that she wouldn't worry so much if he didn't tell her what was bothering him. How wrong he was. As he pulled himself further and further away from the two people he could trust, Alvera became more and more concerned.

One day, Master Marlow and Alvera sat together on the warm sands of the coast. They had been walking through the woods earlier as they did every day and decided to rest down by the shore. It was sunset. The sun's dying embers of crimson, topaz, amethyst, and gold shimmered across the waves, lighting them with their luminous fire. Cotton candy clouds trimmed in lavender swam in a watercolor sky of rose, violet, and periwinkle. A calm sea breeze rolled over the sands with the tide. It smelled of salt and pine. The sea's breath was like a steamy sauna, lulling the beach and its inhabitants to sleep as the tiny waves lapping the shore played a sweet lullaby. Not another sound besides that peaceful song could be heard for miles around. It was such a tranquil scene. Alvera felt as if she could lie on that beach forever and never grow jaded to its sights, sounds, and smells. She looked over at Master Marlow to see if he was as awed by the scene as she was. Her relaxed face tightened with worry at the sight of him.

The master was not smiling as he had been days before. He simply sat there like a forlorn boulder on the beach, blankly staring out at the endless sea. She turned away and looked back out at the vast ocean before her. Suddenly, the ocean did not seem so warm and comforting. The sun had almost completely dipped below the water's engulfing surface, leaving only faint traces of its glowing fire flickering between the waves. The sea had grown blue and cold. Choppy waves agitated the midnight deep below where there were no stars to brighten its gloom. This blanket of darkness seemed to stretch on and on forever. Alvera suddenly felt insignificant and alone in its massiveness. She realized that this was the same place where she had desperately swum to shore many weeks ago. She had felt just as alone then as she did now. A blast of cold wind raced up the shore. She shivered and pulled her legs closer to her chest. Suddenly, she felt a soothing warmth spread into her left arm. She looked over and saw that Master Marlow had placed his hand there. He was looking at her with fatigued eyes. His face seemed paler and more gaunt than usual, but he still managed a weak smile as if to say, "Are you alright?" She smiled back at him to assure him that she was.

Both returned their gazes to the ocean. That simple touch reminded Alvera that she was not alone. Master Marlow and Felix were there for her. They would all brave the daunting sea together. She wanted to help the master face his sorrow as well, but perhaps this time, it was something he had to overcome himself.

* * *

It was the weekend, and Felix was preparing to go to the village to get some much-needed supplies. As he walked down the upper hall tucking his scarf into the collar of his shirt, Master Marlow emerged from his study and stopped him in his tracks.

"You remember what I discussed with you?" the master quietly asked.

Felix nodded. "Yes, Sir."

"Good. Find out as much information as you can while you're there. I also think it would be a good idea if you took Alvera along with you. She needs to get out of the house. Just make sure she doesn't catch on to your real motives for going into town. I don't want to get her hopes up too much."

Felix nodded again, and the two men headed downstairs.

Alvera was quietly reading in one of the chairs of the den when they reached the main floor. Crossing through the kitchen, Master Marlow approached her. She looked up from her book when he lightly tapped her on the shoulder.

"Alvera," he began, "Felix is going to the village this morning, and I would like for you to accompany him. I think you would enjoy getting out."

"Really?" She asked excitedly as she set her book aside. "I can go?"

Master Marlow nodded. An exuberant smile glowed on Alvera's face. She headed eagerly for the side door where Felix stood before abruptly hesitating. She turned around and slowly walked back to the master. His depression was even more tangible than it had been on the beach. Sorrow warped his entire body, and his dark eyes were dull and lifeless. Alvera had never seen him so sad before. She was worried about him and didn't want to leave him by himself. The master read the concern written across her youthful face and attempted to smile.

"Don't worry about me," he whispered soothingly to her. "I'll be fine. You go and have fun. I'll still be here when you get back."

"Come along, Alvera," Felix called cheerfully from the side door as he finished buttoning up his traveling coat.

She looked at Felix and then back at Master Marlow. The master could tell that she was torn between staying or leaving. Giving a slight nod of his head, he urged, "Go on."

After one last searching look into the master's deep eyes, Alvera reluctantly turned and followed Felix out the door.

As they carefully trekked down the steep hill that Master Marlow's house rested on, Alvera saw a cluster of small cottages lining a narrow street just a short distance below them.

"Is that the village?" she asked as she pointed to the miniature town.

"Yes, it is," replied Felix in his cheerful manner. "It may not seem like much, but trust me. I think you'll find it to be a charming little place."

A charming little place it certainly was! Alvera felt as if she were stepping back in time as she entered the enchanting village, for every cottage, hut, and shop retained its original design. Perhaps this was where Master Marlow found his love for antique living. Each building was brightly decorated with colorful banners and vibrant pots of flowers. Long strings of flags stretched over the street from shop to shop still welcomed late summer tourists. Occasionally, a passing car would give a friendly honk to a neighbor on the street. The villagers themselves were incredibly friendly as well. Everyone had a smile on his face, and almost all the shopkeepers cordially greeted each strolling pedestrian.

As they passed a small flower shop on a corner of the bustling street, a kind-faced woman plucked a daisy out of a bouquet she was arranging and stuck it in Alvera's hair. She didn't know what to say. She had never met such a friendly little town before. At the marketplace, Felix stopped to pick up some produce. The open air under the wooden covering of the market was heavily perfumed with fresh berries, succulent peaches, ripe melons, and juicy apples. A maze of crates bursting with fresh fruits and vegetables composed the many aisles of the market. All around, the atmosphere was resonating with the hum of voracious fruit flies, the laughter of children, and the steady rhythm of genial conversation. The marketplace seemed to be the social center of the little village. It almost felt like a town fair to Alvera.

While the curious girl had been invited to sample a slice of peach, Felix wriggled and twisted his way through the labyrinth of crates and people over to the owner of the market. As the owner rang up the price of the goods, Felix quietly asked if he had heard anything about the recent plane crash. All the owner knew was when the crash happened, where it happened, and how many people had survived. Without the identity of the survivors, it was little information to go on. Thanking the owner, Felix located Alvera, and the two headed on to another part of the village.

The rest of their errands took them to the bakery, the deli, the garden shop, and the pharmacy. All these places had been just as friendly as the rest of the village, but none could give Felix any of the information he was searching for. However, one last stop was left on the list. Felix hoped that better answers would turn up here.

"This is one of my favorite shops of the village," he announced as the two neared a small wooden shack secluded on a knoll away from the rest of the village.

"Alvera, welcome to Knick Knacks and Knickerbock-ers."

Felix walked in the open door, and Alvera followed closely behind. A musty smell like that of Master Mar-low's library instantly filled her nostrils as soon as she entered the small shop. Surrounding her on dozens of shelves and wobbly tables were countless antique items. On the nearest shelf to her left, she saw rows and rows of dusty old books, some of which had cobwebs hanging from them. Next to the books were old ink bottles lined up in rows on a stout table. At the end of the little table was a ceramic jar stuffed with writing quills of all colors and sizes. After the quills were several wooden cubbies packed with rolls of traditional parchment paper. As her curious eyes wandered up the towering, crammed shelves, she spotted something dangling from the ceil-ing. Thousands of metal hooks and nails in the rafters held old iron pots and pans, brass kettles, dated cooking utensils, pitchforks, old lamps, quilts, hand-woven bas-kets...almost anything one could imagine!

While Alvera marveled at the nest of antiques, Fe-lix walked up to the front desk of the shop. A short and plump man clothed in a kale green apron instantly stood up from his squatted position behind the desk. "Well, if it isn't Master Felix himself," the man said with a toothy grin. "I was wondering when my best customer would show his face in here again."

"Yes, I know," agreed Felix. "It has been quite a

while. I've been meaning to come sooner, but I've just been so busy."

"I know how that is. Whew! Are you not hot in that overcoat of yours? It's been a blistering summer season here. I've had a fan going in here every day, and I still have to keep that door open!"

Suddenly, the owner's eyes caught Alvera looking at a box full of oil lamps. "Well now!" he breathed with another toothy grin. "Who's this sweet little filly?"

Felix looked over his shoulder. "Oh, that's Alvera. She's been staying with me for about a month now."

"Relative of yours?"

"What? Oh, no. I found her in the woods one day. She said that she had been separated from her parents, so I've been taking care of her until I can find them."

The owner made a clicking noise with his tongue and shook his shaggy head. "Poor thing. Sad when things like that happen."

He suddenly squinted at Alvera's powdery cape. "Strange, though. I would have thought she was yours with that eccentric taste of hers."

Felix gave a nervous laugh and changed the subject. "Say, Pete. Why don't I introduce you properly to her? Alvera, this is Peter..."

"Oh, pish posh!" Pete interrupted with a wave of his chubby hand. "No need for such formalities. Besides, can't you see the wee thing's enjoying herself? Leave her be. Now, what can I do for ya today?"

"Well, I came by to pick up some more quills. Do you happen to have any?"

"Yup," Pete answered as he vanished into the back room. "Just got a new case today."

After a few noisy minutes of rummaging, he returned with a box of black quills in his brawny arms. He set the box on the desk with a grunt and wiped his brow with the edge of his apron.

"You're about the only one who buys these anymore. And since you're such a good customer, I always keep a good stock of 'em just for you."

"Thanks, Pete. This is great."

"You need any ink to go with 'em?"

"Yes, and a few rolls of parchment if you don't mind."

Pete laid the rest of the items on the desk. "Will that be all for ya, Master Felix?"

"Yes."

"I hope so," Pete retorted as he leaned over the desk to get a better look at Felix's bulging shopping bags. "Looks like you've already bought up half the town!"

A hearty guffaw roared from Pete as he laughed at his own joke. Felix just smiled and shook his head at the comical owner. "Well, you know I like to get all my shopping done whenever I'm out."

Pete couldn't hear Felix over his peals of laughter. Finally, when his chuckling wheezed to a stop, he moved over to the register. As he was about to ring up the items, Pete suddenly stopped. A serious look settled over his broad face. Walking back over to the other end of the desk, he grabbed a newspaper out of a metal rack on the side.

"Since you haven't been here in a while," he began, "I don't know if you ever heard about this. Here. Take a look."

Pete plopped the paper in front of Felix. The butler's eyes grew wide and dilated like a cat's eyes as he began scanning the article. It was titled, "Plane Crash Search Party Turns up Empty." This was it. This was exactly what he had been searching for. If he were going to find out any more information concerning the plane crash and Alvera's parents, it was here. Pete started talking before Felix could ask any questions.

"Yeah, this plane crash happened several weeks ago, but folks are still talking about it. This article just came out this week," he said as he pointed a hairy finger at the front-page picture. "Ya see, when the plane crashed just off the coast here, paramedics, firemen, and police arrived as soon as possible. After searching the plane, they only found three survivors. One of 'em was a businessman from London, and the other two were a husband and wife. They took 'em immediately to the hospital not too far from here. The businessman got the brunt of the crash, but the couple only had a few minor injuries and broken bones. While they were at the hospital, they kept saying something about their daughter. They said that she had survived the crash as well, but according to the paramedics, there were no other survivors. However, because the couple kept insisting that their daughter was alive, a search team was formed to look for the girl. They searched the crash site, all along the coast, in the surrounding woods, and even in the ocean for weeks without finding any trace of the girl."

Pete paused to shake his head. "Poor couple. I think they're simply in a state of denial. If I were the hospital, I would have shipped 'em off to the loony doctor as soon as they were well."

After reading the rest of the article, Felix slowly looked up. Hundreds of questions were racing through his excited mind. "So, when was the couple released from the hospital?"

"Just a few days after they were admitted," replied Pete as he rang up the items on an antique register.

"Where did they go?"

"No one knows. All they said was that they were going to go look for their daughter."

Felix's head drooped after hearing that news. He knew for sure now that Alvera's parents were alive, but he still didn't have a clue of where to begin looking for them. Suddenly, he perked up as another question popped into his mind. "Did any of the articles about the crash mention their names?"

"Nope, but I suspect the press knows. The hospital probably forced 'em to keep their mouths shut to protect the couple's identity. You know...because of the situation and all. Well, here you go, Master Felix. That'll be twenty pounds."

Felix deposited the money in Pete's hands and grabbed his bags. "Thanks again, Pete. And thank you for sharing that article with me."

"Here," he said holding out the paper. "It's yours. Free of charge."

Taking the paper, Felix nodded his thanks to Pete, called to Alvera, and headed out the door. He couldn't wait to tell Master Marlow what he had found out about Alvera's parents. He just hoped that it would be enough to decide what to do next.

CHAPTER 12

"I'm telling you, Sir," Felix insisted. "These have got to be the girl's parents."

As soon as dinner was over and Alvera was occupied, Felix had slipped up to the master's study and had given him the good news he had found out. Master Marlow stood in front of Felix and eyed him suspiciously. "But...no names were mentioned," he said slowly. "Are you certain that these are indeed the girl's parents?"

"Positive," the butler responded confidently. "Look."

Whipping out the newspaper that Pete had given him, he pointed to the beginning of one of the paragraphs of the article. "See? It says right here that the couple claimed that their daughter had survived the crash as well. And now they are out looking for her. What are the chances that another couple and their daughter survived the plane crash and became separated? No further proof is needed. These are Alvera's parents."

Master Marlow stared at the article for a long time before slowly pacing away from it to look out the window. He did not want Felix to see the disappointment etched into the deep creases of his face, for secretly, the master had hoped that the girl's parents were dead. He knew it was a selfish wish, but he just couldn't stand the thought of being parted from her. It felt as if someone were trying to take his new-found daughter away from him. Closing his sad eyes, he took a deep breath.

"So, the girl's parents are alive," he muttered more as a statement than a question.

Felix thought it to be the latter. "Yes!" he exclaimed. "Isn't that wonderful, Sir?"

"Yes," the master replied, drawing out the word.

In his excitement, Felix didn't notice the strange emphasis. He was too busy dreaming of the looks on the parents' faces when they were finally reunited with their daughter. Master Marlow, on the other hand, was consumed with trying to work all this information out in his mind.

Downstairs, Alvera presently emerged from the library. She paused uneasily as she entered the darkened den. It was much too quiet even for Master Marlow, and most of the oil lamps had already been snuffed out. She had been left down there all alone. Had they forgotten she was there? Was it time for bed? It was all extremely bizarre. Looking around to make sure that no one was hiding in the eerie shadows gathering in the den and kitchen, Alvera made her way to the staircase to find Felix. As she quietly climbed the stairs, she noticed that it began to grow brighter. The oil lamp at the top of the stairs had been lit, along with the rest of the lamps lining the upper hall. She slowed her pace as her uneasiness mounted. When she reached the floor of the hall, she abruptly stopped and held her breath. A low mumbling sound was vibrating through the still air.

Like a stealthy cat, Alvera slunk along the hall to find the source of the sound. It grew louder and louder until she could clearly tell that it was the sound of people talking. It was loudest when she was in front of the study, so she quietly tiptoed up to the door as close as she dared. Both Felix and Master Marlow were in there discussing something. She strained her ears to discover what they were talking about. Master Marlow's deep voice suddenly resonated through the door.

"We know they are alive, but where are they now?"

"Well…that's the problem," came Felix's muffled response. "I don't know."

There was a pause. A low rumble from Master Marlow rattled the door. "You don't know?"

"No. But, please, Sir…don't be angry with me. I found out everything I could. No one knows where they are. All I did find out was that as soon as Alvera's parents were released from the hospital, they went out and began searching for her."

Alvera sucked in a silent gasp, and her heartbeat quickened. Her parents were alive! They had been found! And now they were out looking for her! She was frozen in disbelief. As she tried to steady herself, she listened to see what else the two men might say. She heard Master Marlow's voice again.

"I'm not angry with you, Felix. You found out everything you could hope to glean from the village, but all this information still leaves us right where we started. We have no idea where to even begin our search. It's been nearly a month since the crash. The girl's parents could be anywhere by now."

"I know…but it's all we have to go on."

Silence filled the room beyond the door again. The adrenaline racing through Alvera's petrified body was flashing millions of thoughts through her whirling mind. Felix and Master Marlow didn't know what to do next. They were right. Her parents could be anywhere.

They could even be halfway across the country for all she knew! But the time for hesitation was over. Something had to be done now.

Inside the study, Felix watched Master Marlow intently for an answer. His large hand was rubbing his aching forehead as he tried to think of a solution to their dilemma. He had promised Alvera that he would do whatever it took to find her parents, but that promise seemed impossible now. There was no certain route. It just wasn't feasible for him to send Felix wandering all over the country. He could end up making circles around the girl's parents and never even know it. It was a foolish idea, yet it was the first suggestion Felix proposed as the master continued to ponder.

"Master Marlow? If you would be willing, I would gladly go out and search for the girl's parents myself even if it took me to the other side of England."

"No," the master quickly snapped back. "That is neither a wise nor a fair decision. I cannot and will not do that to you, Felix."

The butler nodded solemnly and allowed his master to continue his ponderings without any further interruptions.

Not doing anything about the situation made Master Marlow feel guilty. He felt as if he were breaking his promise and possibly his trust with Alvera, and the last thing he wanted was to lose her trust. She relied on him so much. He just couldn't do that to her. A new thought suddenly appeared in the master's throbbing mind. Perhaps there was a way to keep his promise to Alvera even if he couldn't get out there to look for her parents himself. Looking up with his newborn idea twinkling in his eyes, Master Marlow turned to the expectant butler. "Felix, I think the best way to find the girl's parents is to let them find us."

The butler cocked his curly head in confusion as if the master had lost his mind.

"What I mean," he explained, "is if we go out to look for the girl's parents, we'll all be running circles around each other, and that won't get us anywhere. By staying put, the girl's parents will hopefully find their way here to their daughter. In other words, there is a greater chance of her parents finding us than of us finding them."

Felix finally understood and nodded in agreement. "If that is what you think is best, that is fine with me. However, if we are just going to wait here for Alvera's parents to show up, could I do one thing?"

"What?"

"I would at least like to go to the hospital to inquire about the girl's parents to see if I can find out anything else."

Master Marlow conceded to Felix's wishes.

"You may go if it will make you feel better, but remember what I told you. The hospital may not be willing to release any information to those outside the immediate family."

"I know, but it won't hurt to try."

With that, Felix quietly turned toward the door and left Master Marlow to his thoughts. As he headed downstairs, he realized just how late it was. It was about time he tucked Alvera in bed. He went straight to the library where he had left her last.

"Alvera," he softly called. "Why don't you come upstairs, and I'll put you to bed?"

There was no response. Perhaps she had fallen asleep. Felix quietly entered the library and called her name again. "Alvera."

He scanned the shadows of the octagonal room for a sleeping figure, but all the chairs and corners were completely empty. He paused to think for a moment. If Alvera had become sleepy, perhaps she had already retired to her bedroom for the night. Retracing his steps, he headed back upstairs to make sure she was alright. Upon opening her bedroom door, however, Felix started to worry. The bed didn't have a single wrinkle in the covers. She hadn't come to bed. As he slowly closed the door, another idea popped into his head. Perhaps she was in the bathroom. He hurried down the hall and knocked on the bathroom door. No answer. He jiggled the handle. The unlocked door opened easily. Now Felix really started to panic. Where could she be?

He galloped back downstairs and searched every room, closet, and corner. He even checked the library again. Alvera was nowhere to be found down there. Felix sprinted back upstairs, his heart now pounding against his chest. Frantically, he flung open every door. Each room turned up empty.

Hearing all the commotion, Master Marlow stepped out of his study. He was met with a panic-stricken butler pacing the hallway. He looked as if he were about ready to yank all his curly hair out. "Felix, what on earth are you doing out here? It sounds as if a stampede were running about the house."

"I'm sorry, Sir," Felix shakily apologized. "I didn't mean to disturb you. It's just that...I can't find Alvera anywhere."

Master Marlow looked at him sharply. "What do you mean?"

"That's exactly what I mean! She's gone, Sir!"

A look of concern covered the master's face like a mask as he realized that the distressed butler wasn't joking. He closed the door to his study and proceeded down the hall. Felix jogged closely behind the master's heels.

"Have you looked everywhere in the house?" asked Master Marlow.

"Yes, I've searched every room. Some of them more than once."

"Not every room," corrected the master as he stopped in front of the door to the forbidden room. Pulling a key out of his cloak, he twisted it in the lock and opened the door enough to poke his head in. He quickly glanced around the room, but Alvera was not there. Felix peered curiously around the master, for he had never been allowed to see the forbidden room before.

"What is that, Sir?"

"Never mind, Felix," Master Marlow curtly replied as he forcefully closed the door and locked it.

Stuffing the key back in his cloak, he hurriedly trotted downstairs with Felix trailing behind. It was exceedingly dark and difficult to identify things, but there was just enough golden light flooding down the stairs for the master to make out a cluttered heap suspiciously resting on the kitchen table. Grabbing a candle from one of the shelves in the kitchen, he lit it and approached the messy pile. Wadded up blankets, apples, bananas, peaches, and a pair of scissors were all haphazardly piled together in a heap on the table. At the sight of these sundry items, Master Marlow feared that he knew what they meant, but before he could make this conclusion, he had to be sure.

"Felix," he said slowly.

"Yes, Sir?"

"Did you happen to leave all this stuff here?"

"No, Sir, I didn't. In fact, I didn't even notice it until you pointed it out."

The master's worst fears were confirmed. He knew what he had to do. Still holding the candle, he stalked over to the side door.

"Alvera must have overheard our conversation," he said as he grabbed a lantern hanging on a hook by the door. "Now, she has run away to find her parents."

Felix's mouth dropped open in shock. He wanted to say something, but he couldn't find his voice. Once Master Marlow had lit the lantern and exited through the door, the stunned butler finally regained his voice along with his feet.

"Sir!" he cried as he ran to the door. "Wait! What are you doing? Where are you going?"

"I'm going to find her," the master curtly replied without looking back. "And do not follow me, Felix. I need you to stay here."

The master had just reached the iron gate when Felix called out to him again from the door.

"But, Sir! The village!"

For the first time in his haste, Master Marlow stopped. He knew what Felix meant. The master had not left his property in nearly twenty years. This would be his first time returning to the village, and he would be deceiving himself if he didn't admit that he was terrified about it. But his love for Alvera outweighed his fears. He had no choice.

Lowering his head and closing his eyes in submission, the master replied in a low voice, "I know." Without further hesitation, he vanished beyond the gate and the barricade of trees into the unknown.

CHAPTER 13

The only sound Alvera could hear was the hurried pattering of her own feet. It was an eerily quiet night. Not even the crickets dared to chirp their midnight lullaby. The uneasiness of the silence caused her to question what she was doing. Maybe she shouldn't have made the rash decision of searching for her parents in the dark alone. But she had already made it past the village and the hospital. It was too late to turn back now, so she pressed on as bravely as she could. She was traveling along a dirt road that was closely hemmed in by dense woods on either side. There were no houses or shops along this road, but Alvera kept the hood of her cloak up, just in case someone should come along. She didn't want anyone to recognize her. The night had been dark when she had first set out, but the surrounding woods made it even more obscure. She could barely make out the silhouettes of her feet and nearly tripped over several tree roots that jutted across her path. A chilly wind swept through the tunnel of trees. She pulled the edges of her cloak more tightly around her. She was glad that she had decided to take it with her. She hadn't realized what a cold night it was going to be.

Just as the wind had blown its frigid breath, it ceased. All the leaves were held still on their branches as the maze of trees fell limp. Nothing moved except for Alvera. It was as if the whole world had been frozen in time. She had never felt so alone. Suddenly, she wished that were true. As she continued her quest, Alvera noticed that the treading of her feet sounded faster than they were actually moving. She stopped. The other scuffling stopped. Her heart began to beat faster. Someone or something was following her. Without moving her head, she scanned each side of the woods. It was nothing but darkness and shadows. She would never be able to see what was truly there in these gloomy conditions.

Feeling as if something were going to jump out at her at any minute, Alvera decided that it would be better if she kept moving. But as soon as she resumed walking, that echoing pace began trailing her again, more closely. Involuntarily, she quickened her pace as her adrenaline started to flow. If only she had stayed in the doctor's house! She would have had nothing to fear there. But now she was fearing for her life, and there was no one around to help her.

Alvera was suddenly roused from her frantic thoughts when a second scampering noise raced past her and rattled the bushes and tall blades of unkempt grass. The flailing of the disturbed shrubbery stopped a short distance in front of her. Not wanting to encounter what was hiding in those bushes, Alvera abruptly halted. She jumped and turned her head in all directions as more scuttling feet shook the woods on either side.

Once the initial rush ceased, the petrified girl's assassins stealthily crept closer to her. Her wide eyes desperately attempted to pierce the darkness that was engulfing her to identify her captors, but it was no use. She could only hear the ever-nearing rustling of grass and snapping of twigs. Alvera had been aware of her heavy breathing ever since she realized that she was being followed, but she hadn't realized how loud it had been. However, it was not her breath that she was hearing. Low, raspy breaths were rattling in front of and beside her. It was as if the woods themselves were closing her in with their cacophonous lungs. She could almost feel the humid heat of their breath clinging to her skin.

Suddenly, she spotted a slinking figure slowly emerging from the woods in front of her. Two luminous eyes glowed from its shadowed face as it turned to face her. Alvera's pounding heart quivered in the depths of her stomach when she realized what the figure was. A wolf. But not just one wolf. She was surrounded by a whole pack of wolves.

Now the frightened girl really started to panic. She couldn't run. Any sudden move would launch the hungry wolves into action, and they could easily over-take her. But she couldn't just stand motionless forever either. The wolves were already starting to form a tight-er circle around her. Menacing growls rumbled in their throats. What was she going to do? Remembering her sack of supplies that she had tossed over her shoulder, Alvera swung it around and quickly rummaged through its contents. She yanked out a few slices of bread, broke them into smaller pieces, and began tossing them to the ravenous wolves. The snarling phantoms instantly pounced upon the bread pieces and tore at them as if they were a dead carcass. These wolves must have been starving. Alvera hoped that by giving them the bread, she could appease their hunger a bit and possibly es-cape. However, the clamoring wolves scarfed the mor-sels down so quickly that she could barely tear another piece off before they had finished the first! Not all the wolves were getting an equal share of the bread either. Those unfortunate members of the pack continued to stealthily hem the terrified girl in as they glared at her with hungry eyes. This plan wasn't working. If the whole pack was not preoccupied, there was no chance of her escaping.

Alvera tossed another piece of the bread and began to tear off another piece when she realized that she had run out. All the wolves looked at her with expectant eyes and began to approach her more quickly and bold-ly. Terrified, Alvera frantically threw the apples, peaches, and bananas she had in her sack into the thickest cluster of the wolves. She knew it wouldn't suffice their hunger, but it was all that she had left. The fruits didn't even phase the persistent wolves. They merely sniffed at them as they continued to advance on the poor girl. She knew that she needed to stand her ground, but she was shaking so badly that her buckling knees began to propel her backwards. Seeing her involuntary attempt to flee, one of the wolves ran behind her, grabbed the hood of her cloak, and yanked her to the ground. The moment she hit the dirt, Alvera knew that it was over. With one swift movement, the entire pack lunged toward her. *This is it!* she thought hysterically to herself. *I'm going to die! I'm going to die!* The wolf that had turned to face her before the others emerged suddenly charged through the rest of the pack and leaped at the helpless girl sprawled on her back. The whole scene felt as if it were in slow motion as she stared wide-eyed into the gaping mouth full of glimmering fangs descending upon her. Covering her face with her arms and squeezing her eyes shut, Alvera screamed as she braced herself for the inevitable.

"GET AWAY FROM HER!!!" thundered a booming voice.

The terrified girl felt a gust of wind sweep over her and heard a painful yelp. Tentatively, she opened her eyes and lowered her arms. Standing protectively in front of her was a dark, caped figure that she recognized immediately. It was Master Marlow! He had come to rescue her! The agonized cry that she had heard had come from the wolf that had been leaping toward her. Master Marlow had knocked him to the ground with a forceful blow. As the stunned wolf scrambled back to his feet, the rest of the pack gathered around him to face their new attacker as one. Their snarls and growls were more ferocious than they had been before as they stealthily advanced toward the master. Several of the incensed wolves even flashed their dagger-like fangs and bristled their matted fur in an intimidating manner.

But Master Marlow was not afraid. He swung a lantern that he was carrying back and forth in front of the vicious wolves. Slightly unnerved, they backed off a bit with agitated snorts and yaps. Amazed by the wolves' reactions, Alvera slowly stood to her feet to get a better view of what was happening. The wolves had retreated about a foot away before they decided to hold their ground. They were far enough away to where the swinging light no longer felt threatening to them. Seeing this boundary, Master Marlow suddenly smashed the lantern on the ground. The oil inside the lantern splashed onto the flame and caused a bright explosion. Orange flames roared and leaped into the air, and several glowing sparks crackled, popped, and flew at the bewildered wolves. Several of the wolves on the front line of the pack were so alarmed by the sudden blaze that they scampered off into the woods. Only a few of the menacing beasts remained.

Spreading his cloak wide like a pair of bat wings to triple his size, Master Marlow took a deep breath and let out a gut-wrenching roar. Alvera covered her ears. That roar was unlike any that she had ever heard before. It sounded like some monstrous, demonic beast howling out in a harangue of pure anger. Whatever it resembled, it worked to scare away the wolves once and for all. With tails tucked between their flailing legs, the last of the wolves vanished into the obscure woods.

Master Marlow slowly allowed his cloak to fall back to his sides. He stared into the shadows where the wolves had disappeared for a long while to make sure they didn't come back. Once he was certain that they were gone, he turned to face Alvera. By that time, the miniature bonfire of the broken lantern had smoldered into embers, preventing her from seeing the master's face clearly. However, she did not want to see his face. She could not look at his face, for she did not want to see the scolding look of hurt and misunderstanding that she just knew was there. She lowered her head as tears began to well up in her eyes. Her guilt from running away was almost as unbearable as the convicting silence of the master. He loved her and had done so much for her, and how had she repaid him? By running away. He wouldn't understand. He would think that she did not care for him. His new-found trust would be broken. Maybe he wouldn't even give the world another chance after what she had done to him. It broke Alvera's heart to think about all this. She wanted to tell him why she had run away. She wanted to tell him that it wasn't because she didn't like being with him. She wanted to tell him how thankful she was that he had saved her from the wolves. She wanted to tell him that she loved him like her own father. But the growing lump in her throat prevented her from doing so.

In a tiny trembling voice, all Alvera managed to squeak was, "I'm sorry." More silence was her only response. The tears began to roll down her cheeks. What had she been thinking? She had only been thinking about herself and not about how her actions would affect the master. Alvera feared that he would never trust her again, but she didn't blame him. She didn't deserve his trust.

Suddenly, a gentle hand touched her chin and slowly raised her drooping head. Alvera found herself looking up into the master's face. Even though most of it was obscured in shadows, Alvera could clearly see his deep eyes. Within the pools of black, she saw a glimmer of love slowly brighten. It was a warm, caring look that touched her heart. There was no need for her to explain. He understood. A watery smile flickered across her face before she broke down in a flood of tears. Picking up the shattered remains of the lantern and wrapping them in Alvera's sack, Master Marlow walked over to her side.

"Come on," he whispered soothingly. "Let's go home."

Alvera nodded as the bitter tears continued to flow. Wrapping a portion of his cloak tenderly around her, Master Marlow led her down the path.

CHAPTER 14

Not once since the incident did anyone mention it. The days simply passed on as they had before. It was as if that terrible night had never happened. Alvera was very grateful for the master's forgiveness and understanding. It made the whole situation much easier to handle, for her tender conscience still stung every time she thought of that night. The day after she had tried to run away, Felix journeyed up to the hospital that Alvera's parents had been taken to a few miles away from the village. Just as Master Marlow had warned, the medical staff was unwilling to give Felix any personal information concerning the girl's parents. However, the staff did sympathize with him and agreed to tell him what they could. The couple had left the hospital in good condition and said that they were going to find their little girl. That was all the hospital knew outside of the couple's personal information. Just like everyone else, they had no clue as to where they could be. It was a disappointing outcome, but Felix, as well as the master, had expected it to be so. However, it wasn't a pointless inquiry. At least now they knew that they had done everything they could to locate the girl's parents. All they could hope for now was that they would somehow find their way here.

Several days after Felix's trip to the hospital, Master Marlow decided to have a picnic. He knew that Alvera would enjoy that very much. On an old blanket spread beneath the shade of the poplar tree sat the three of them together. A light breeze whistling through the flapping leaves of the trees made the summer day cool and relaxing. Puffy cumulus clouds sailed swiftly through the sky, casting their huge shadows over the rippling grass. They almost appeared to be animals crawling beneath the earth causing the grass to roll. All around, the yard echoed with the rushing current of the wind, the hissing of the shaking leaves, and the occasional peeping of a bird. It was such a tranquil day.

After they had finished eating their picnic lunch, Felix took the dishes and empty containers back inside. Alvera stared up at the swift clouds as she sipped her lemonade. Her dreamy thoughts drifted along with them. Master Marlow sat up from leaning against the trunk of the poplar to gaze at the clouds as well. He took a deep breath and sighed. "It's a beautiful day, isn't it?" he softly spoke.

"It is," Alvera replied with a nod.

The master looked over at her with a serious expression. He too had been deeply lost in his thoughts. "Alvera…do you still think about your parents?"

Surprised by his question, she turned toward him with a slightly confused look on her face. Her expression said, "Of course I still think about my parents." But Alvera merely nodded.

"I know you must miss them terribly," the master continued almost in a reverie. "Please believe me when I say this. Felix and I have done everything we possibly can to find your parents. We now know that it is illogical for us to go out and search for them ourselves. At this point, we are simply hoping that they will find us. Please don't think that I'm giving up. That's the last thing I would ever do. My promise still stands firm. You may stay here until your parents are found."

Alvera smiled at the master. She realized that he was just trying to reassure her and comfort her. Master Marlow saw her sweet smile and lowered his gaze bashfully. Oh, how he loved her! He wished that she could stay with him forever. He wanted to watch her grow and experience the joy of raising a child. Combing his slicked-back hair nervously with his fingers, Master Marlow tried to figure out how to express this wish to Alvera.

"And if…for some reason…you never find your parents…you are always…welcome…to stay here…with me."

To the stuttering doctor's surprise, Alvera suddenly leaned across the blanket and wrapped her tiny arms around him.

"Thank you so much!" she exclaimed. "You are so kind! I would love to stay here with you. I know that you would take good care of me."

Master Marlow's heart was flooded with warmth and joy. That was all he had wanted to hear. If her parents were never found, she would stay here with him, and he would never have to lose her. Never. Wrapping his own arms around Alvera, Master Marlow pulled her closer as if he were afraid of someone snatching her away from him.

After they had released each other, Felix came hobbling out the side door, awkwardly struggling to carry a bulky piece of equipment. "Master Marlow!" he gasped as he staggered toward them. "Look what I found!"

Wobbling to a halt, the tuckered butler clumsily set his prize on the ground. It was a rickety wooden stand with a camera precariously balanced on top. It looked like a dusty piece of junk covered in cobwebs, but Felix was smiling so widely that one would have guessed it to be a precious treasure.

Master Marlow, however, was not impressed. "Felix," he began with a reproachful scowl, "where did you get that?"

"Oh, I got this years ago at an old camera store. They offered me the camera at a great bargain and gave me the stand for free. I just couldn't pass it up. I've always wanted to use it, and I thought today would be the perfect day."

The master's scowl deepened.

"Felix, you know how I feel about pictures."

"I know, Sir. But this is a special moment. I just thought it would be nice to have a photo to remember it."

The master was about to argue the matter further when Alvera placed a gentle hand on his own. He looked at her. An imploring look swam in the ocean of her eyes, and her mouth softly smiled in a soothing way. Master Marlow's indignation cooled at the sight of her sweet face and glowing hair. She always knew how to calm him down, even without speaking. He would miss that quality when she was gone. Pondering on that fact, the master decided that perhaps it would not be such a bad idea to take a picture today, for there was no guarantee that Alvera would be with him forever. Besides, he needed to overcome his troubled past of portraits.

"Alright," Master Marlow sighed as he got to his feet. "Just this once."

"Oh! Thank you, Sir!" Felix shouted excitedly with a giddy little jump. "Thank you!"

Immediately, he began setting the wobbly stand up; however, it turned out to be more of a fight instead. None of the legs of the wooden stand wanted to hold firm. They all kept collapsing in on each other. The camera was also throwing fits. It kept spinning on its perch in every direction except the one in which Felix wanted it to go. After much fidgeting and struggling, however, the persistent butler finally managed to set the stand and camera up straight.

"Alright," he breathed. "It's ready. You two go stand over there, and I'll make sure everything's lined up."

Master Marlow and Alvera walked in front of the camera and stood next to each other while Felix checked the screen.

"Perfect," he said satisfactorily as he jogged back around the camera.

Grabbing a small remote attached to the camera by a thin wire, Felix made his way over to Master Marlow and Alvera.

"Alright. On the count of three, everybody smile. One...two...three!"

Felix mashed the button on the remote a little too hard, and the camera blinded the three of them with two dazzling flashes. Bright lights flickered before all their stunned eyes. Apparently unaware of his mishap, Felix eagerly rushed over to the camera to catch the picture as it came out. As soon as the blobs of light vanished from her eyes and she could see the master's irate expression clearly, Alvera giggled. Seeing the humor in the whole situation, Master Marlow soon found himself chuckling a bit too. Alvera's laughter was always contagious. While Felix waited for the picture to develop, the two of them sat back down on the blanket and sipped on their lemonade. It truly was a beautiful day. If only it could last forever.

Suddenly, Alvera jerked her head toward the front gate of the property. She was staring intently at something. Master Marlow was going to ask her what the matter was when she suddenly sprang to her feet with her mouth gaping in amazement. She couldn't believe what she was seeing. Could it be? Was it really true? Two figures were slowly rising over the top of the hill just in front of the gate. They were too far away to distinguish, but evidently, Alvera didn't need any details to know who they were. Breaking into a run, she raced toward the approaching strangers. Master Marlow rose to his feet in alarm and stared after her. But the longer he stared, the less wary he became. A deep sorrow replaced his initial apprehensions. The time had come before he was ready. Then again, would he ever be ready?

Unaware of what was going on, Felix walked over to the numb master waving two dark pieces of paper in his hand.

"Well, it turns out I accidentally took two pictures," he explained, "but they came out great. Here you are, Sir."

Master Marlow took the pictures from Felix without really looking at them. He couldn't take his eyes off Alvera.

"What's the matter, Sir?" Felix asked, noticing the master's distracted look.

Turning his head in the direction that Master Marlow was gazing, Felix spotted the two strangers. A sharp pang of fear stabbed his stomach.

"Oh, dear. I must have forgotten to close the gate last night. I'm terribly sorry, Sir. Please don't be angry with me. I ..."

He paused in his apology when he noticed the master's blank look. It appeared as if he hadn't heard a word of what Felix had just said.

"Sir?" he quietly questioned with concern. "Are you alright? Who is that?"

Master Marlow still made no response, so Felix decided that it was best to stop talking. The two simply stared on in silence, waiting to see what would happen.

Alvera ran up to the two figures and gave them a hug. The three of them stayed in that embracing position for several minutes. When they finally broke away from each other, it appeared as if they began talking. During their conversation, Alvera turned back and pointed at Master Marlow and Felix. The two strangers looked in that direction as well. Eagerly, she motioned for them to follow her, and the three of them slowly made their way across the lawn. As they drew closer, the perplexed butler began to understand who the strangers were. It was a husband and wife. The wife was a tall and slender woman with long, flowing chestnut hair. Her elegant face was speckled with an array of merry freckles, and two brown, doe-like eyes glistened with joyful tears. She limped slightly as she walked because of a boot on her left leg. She leaned on her husband who was an equally tall spouse with a strong body. His sandy hair and mustache were slightly darker than Alvera's golden waves, but his crystal blue eyes were nearly identical to hers. There was no doubt about it. Alvera's parents had finally found their lost daughter.

The family paused just a few feet in front of Master Marlow and Felix. Stepping forward, Alvera broke the strange silence. "Mom, Dad, this is Mr. Marlow and Mr. Felix. They're the ones who rescued me."

Alvera's mother stepped forward as renewed tears of joy trickled from her eyes. "Thank you so much for caring for our daughter," she softly uttered with deep emotion. "How can we ever repay you?"

Seeing that she wanted to give him a hug, Master Marlow took a step back and held up his hands.

"No," he replied gravely. "You have no need to give me anything. Your daughter's company over the past several weeks is payment enough."

He paused for a moment as he pondered on something.

"All I ask…is that Alvera be allowed to visit me."

Grateful smiles glowed on each of the overjoyed parents' faces. Alvera's father nodded in response to the master's request. "Certainly," he replied. "We would love for our daughter to be able to visit you as often as she can, and I know Alvera would greatly enjoy that as well."

She looked up at her father with an exuberant smile and loving eyes and nodded vigorously.

"Thank you again," her mother choked out.

The master simply nodded.

Placing their arms around their precious daughter, Alvera's parents escorted her back toward the gate. Halfway across the lawn, she turned to her parents, asked them to wait, and raced back to Master Marlow and Felix. Felix, tears already streaming down his elongated face, squatted down and caught Alvera in his open arms.

"Oh! I'm going to miss you, Alvera," he said in a quavering voice. "You've brought so much joy to this place. We'll never forget you. Take care of yourself, dear."

Alvera nodded with a smile at Felix before sprinting over to Master Marlow. She wrapped him in a tight hug and rested her head against his chest. In return, the master folded his arms around her frail body and nestled his face in her golden hair. It smelled of fresh grass and wildflowers. As he stood there embracing her, he felt something welling up inside him that he had never felt before. It felt as if his sorrow were pushing a swelling wave of water up his throat, but a lump that had already formed there prevented the wave from rising any further. Unable to release itself, the rushing tide raced throughout the rest of the master's body.

What was wrong with him? Why did he feel this way? Alvera must have been experiencing the same overwhelming feeling, for a pool of sparkling tears floated on the brim of her eyelids. "I'm going to miss you," she whispered as she buried her head further into his chest.

"And I will miss you," the master softly replied. "But it is time for you to return home with your family. Here."

He handed Alvera the extra picture that Felix had accidentally taken and took out his own. "Now I will always be with you, and you will always be with me."

A watery smile glowed on Alvera's face as her tears spilled over. Grasping her picture, she hugged the master even tighter.

"Thank you so much for everything. I promise that

I'll visit as often as I can, and when I can't come, I'll write to you."

Master Marlow folded his arms back around her slender shoulders and closed his eyes. He knew that she would keep her promise just as he had kept his.

"I love you, Mr. Marlow."

Those simple words stirred the master's flood into a raging hurricane that threatened to overpower him. He gulped trying to restrain the whipping waters as he struggled to process all these unfamiliar emotions. Alvera's love for him had grown so strong that he had become a second father to her. And when he thought about it, the master had grown to love Alvera as if she were his own daughter. Now that he was being separated from her, he was feeling the full force of his suppressed emotions. This day had never seemed possible to him, but now he had to accept that it was the reality of the situation. And oh, how it hurt his sensitive heart! It was agony! He didn't want to lose his precious girl, but he realized that by keeping her to himself, he would be hurting her. In that moment, he finally understood why Alvera had released the little insects that she had cared for. Because she loved them. Now it was his turn to let her go.

Controlling his voice as best he could, Master Marlow whispered, "I love you too ... Alvera."

After holding her in his arms for a few moments longer, he reluctantly released her. Smiling one last time at the doctor, Alvera turned and slowly walked back to her parents. Both Master Marlow and Felix watched the reunited family shrink into the distance. When they reached the gate, they were no bigger than a cluster of flowers. But before they completely vanished, Alvera turned and waved a final farewell. Master Marlow raised his hand to wave back, but he could not bring himself to look at Alvera and her family any longer. His flood of emotions was about to break the dam that had been lodged in his throat, and he did not want anyone to see. Wrapping his cloak protectively around himself, he quickly bolted for the side door. Felix did not notice the master's hasty exit, for he was still waving after Alvera even once she was out of sight. Taking a deep breath and wiping the tears from his eyes, he turned to talk to the master.

"Oh, isn't it wonder..."

Realizing that he was talking to the air, the bewildered butler spun in a circle looking for Master Marlow. "Sir?"

Suddenly, Felix spotted the hem of the master's cape whipping through the side door of the house. He ran to catch up with him. By the time he stampeded into the kitchen, Master Marlow was already halfway up the stairs.

"Sir!" he cried. "Where are you going?"

The master paused on the stairs. Grasping the rail to steady himself, he took a shuddering breath and spoke as calmly as he could. "I'm going upstairs for a while, Felix. I...I need to be alone. Don't bother with checking on me. In fact, you don't ever have to worry about assisting me again. I set you free as my butler."

Felix's mouth dropped open and nearly hit his chest. He was at a loss for words. Was the master feeling well? Did he really say what Felix thought he just said? Seeing the master continue his retreat up the stairs, Felix finally found his voice. "But, Sir...what am I supposed to do?"

"It does not matter to me," Master Marlow curtly replied. "Just...leave me alone."

With that, he mounted the rest of the stairs, marched down the hall, and locked himself in the forbidden room, leaving the stunned butler alone.

Leaning against the closed door, Master Marlow breathed heavily as if he had been wounded. The raging waters tore at his insides, yet he still tried to fight them off. Taking a few halting steps forward, he staggered toward the mirrors on the far side of the room. He stopped abruptly in front of them and clenched the left side of his chest. It felt as if his heart were being ripped out of his flesh. What was happening to him? Without warning, the lump in his throat sunk into the churning waters, and the waves surged upward. His breath caught in the drowning waters. He looked up. Reflected in the mirrors was a man he knew very well, but at that moment, he could barely recognize him. His sensitive side had been exposed, and the master felt extremely vulnerable, even though he was alone. He struggled with himself. He couldn't allow such weakness to overcome him. He had to be strong, just as he had been for Alvera.

Alvera! But she was gone now. He had nothing to stand up for. No one to comfort. No one to lean on. He was alone, and he couldn't win the battle he was so desperately fighting. The waters forced their way up to his head, causing it to throb with pain as the pressure began to build. For a moment, there did not seem to be a way of escape, but as the agitated waters continued to swirl around, they found the master's weak spot. Master Marlow squeezed his eyes shut as the waters caused them to burn. It felt as if lava were being poured into his eyes. Suddenly, the intense burning ceased and was replaced with a soothing warmth that spread onto the master's cheek. He opened his eyes and looked back at his reflection. Glistening on his face from the corner of one of his pink eyes was a solitary tear. He reached up to touch his cheek and was surprised to find that it was wet. What was wrong with him? He had never felt anything like this before. It was all so overwhelming. Before he could stop them, more tears trickled from his eyes. For the first time that he could ever recollect, Master Marlow wept like a child.

His vision blurred as the bitter tears flowed forth in a rapid cascade. Banging a fist against one of the mirrors, Master Marlow slowly sunk to his knees. When he reached the floor, his weeping turned into sobbing. He pressed his pounding head against the silver panes and gnashed his teeth in agony. His heart-wrenching sobs shook his sagging shoulders violently. *Please*, he pleaded to God, *let this stop! I cannot bear this pain any longer! Please help me!* But the tears continued to pour out relentlessly. In his bitter anguish, Master Marlow could not take his thoughts off Alvera. She had been such a sweet companion to him. Eager to learn. Eager to help. And she had one of the most caring hearts that the master had ever seen. Even when he had been cruel to her, she had still cared about him. She had taught him so much. How to smile. How to laugh. How to change. How to love. He had been motivated to get up each day just to see her beautiful face.

But that face would no longer greet him each morning. It had left him, and he feared that his new-found love had flown away with it. But if his love were gone, why did he care so much about her absence? In that moment, Master Marlow realized that his love along with all the other things he had learned had not abandoned him. And Alvera had not either. He simply had to lose the presence of the one he loved to realize that she would always be with him in his heart.

Slowly, his choking sobs subsided into a few remaining tears. Reaching into the depths of his cloak, Master Marlow pulled out the picture of him standing with Alvera and Felix. He wiped away the last of his tears with the edge of his cloak and smiled as he gazed at the precious portrait. A lightness filled his heart and began to mend his emotional scars. He had released all his sorrow and anguish that he had locked away inside himself for so long, and he felt as if he had been cleansed. There was no reason for him to be sad anymore, for it wouldn't do him any good. And Alvera certainly wouldn't want him to spend his days in sorrow.

From that day forward, Master Marlow promised to act on what Alvera had taught him and to cherish her love for him, even when she was not with him. Besides, God loved him as well, and if Master Marlow would simply remember that, he would never feel alone.

CHAPTER 15

Early the next morning, Master Marlow emerged from the forbidden room feeling refreshed and determined to make a change. His eyes and cheeks were still slightly puffy and sticky from crying so much, so he went to the bathroom and splashed some cold water on his face. Once he had dried himself off, he headed down the hall toward the stairs. Rather abruptly, the master halted on the top step. At the bottom of the stairs, a bashful-looking Felix smiled up at him.

"Good morning, Sir," he said in his cheery manner. "Would you care for some breakfast?"

Master Marlow stared at Felix in confusion. "What are you doing here?" he quietly asked, not unkindly.

Felix shyly looked at the floor and twisted his foot into the wood. "Well, I know you gave me permission to leave, Sir, but I just couldn't bring myself to do it. This is my home. My place is here serving you. But you are not just my master; you are my friend, Master Marlow Sir."

A stoic expression rested on Master Marlow's face which caused Felix's hopeful smile to fade. He couldn't tell whether the master approved of his decision or not. Averting his gaze, Master Marlow slowly trudged down the steps. With each step he took, Felix grew more and more nervous. He expected many things from the master, but he did not expect what happened next. When he reached the bottom of the staircase, Master Marlow looked at Felix for a moment before enveloping him in a hug. The startled butler stiffened in the master's tight grip, unable to move. However, as the strangeness of Master Marlow's behavior wore off, Felix relaxed and hugged him back. Stepping back, the master placed his hands on Felix's shoulders and looked him in the eyes with a grateful smile.

"Thank you, Felix," he said in a warm voice. "I'm glad you didn't listen to me and decided to stay. I did not realize just how important your company is to me."

Felix nodded with a wide grin. "I'm glad to be here, Sir."

Tossing an arm over Master Marlow's broad shoulders, Felix led him into the kitchen for breakfast. Both were now closer friends than they ever had been before.

* * *

"Felix," Master Marlow muttered nervously, "I don't know if I can do this. It's a little too much too soon."

A new day had dawned, and before the crowds flooded in, Felix had decided to take Master Marlow a little way into the village. They had already descended the hill, and the master was becoming increasingly anxious the farther away they walked.

Ignoring the master's qualms, Felix cheerily replied, "Nonsense, Sir! This is good for you. Besides, I think you'll find that you have a lot in common with the person I'm going to introduce you to today."

Soon, the valley below the hill branched off in two directions. The flat path led into the heart of the village while a steeper path veered up a hill to the left. Felix led Master Marlow up the latter path. While the master was relieved that they would not be travelling into the main part of the village, he was still extremely anxious about encountering even a remote villager. Seeing the peak of a roof beginning to protrude from the top of the hill as they continued to climb, Master Marlow pulled his hood over his head. Almost as if he sensed what the master was doing, Felix snapped his head around to confront him. "Don't even think about it."

He slowed his pace until he was beside Master Marlow and yanked his hood off his head.

"There's nothing to be afraid of, Sir. You've been to the village before."

"Yes," the master agreed. "But that was at night. This is during broad daylight. There is a big difference, Felix."

"You're right," he concurred with a smug grin. "There is a big difference this time."

Master Marlow looked curiously at Felix. He was waiting for an explanation.

Looking back at the master out of the corners of his eyes, Felix replied, "*I'm* right here beside you."

Despite his nervousness, Master Marlow couldn't help but smile at Felix's cleverness. He was right. It was time for him to confront one of his biggest fears, but he wouldn't have to do it alone.

Finally, they arrived at the top of the hill. The tip of the roof had now expanded into a small shack. *Well, at least it's only one shop*, the master thought reassuringly to himself. As they approached the tiny shop, Master Marlow noticed the wooden sign hanging above the door: Kick Knacks and Knickerbockers. So, this was the old antique store that Felix always talked about. It had a much different name and location than the one the master had visited twenty years ago, but perhaps it would be just as nice. Felix certainly always bought fine quills from this place.

The butler waltzed right into the quaint little shop as if it were a second home to him, but Master Marlow hesitated. Cautiously, he peeked around the corners of the door frame. There were no other customers in sight. Taking a deep breath, he took an exaggerated step over the threshold to force himself to go in. The master found himself surrounded by antiques of all shapes and sizes.

He almost felt as if he had stepped into his own home. The place even smelled like his home! But he would not allow himself to become too comfortable in the shop. After all, he was not in the security of his own house.

The master looked up to see where Felix had wandered off to. He was already at the front desk chatting away with the owner. Hoping to go unnoticed, Master Marlow began to slink toward a shadowed corner of the shop, but to his horror, Felix turned around and gestured in his direction.

"Pete, I'd like to introduce you to a dear friend of mine. This is Malcus Marlow."

There was nothing the master could do to escape now. Reluctantly, he shuffled toward the front desk.

"Well, Master Malcus," Pete warmly greeted with his toothy grin, "the name's Pete. Nice to meet you."

He extended a hairy hand, and Master Marlow tentatively shook it.

"It's a pleasure to meet you as well," the master mumbled without meaning it.

Still smiling broadly, Pete began a light conversation. "So, where're ya from, Master Malcus?"

"Well, I actually live right here in the village."

Pete's bushy eyebrows rose in surprise. "Ya don't say? How long have you lived here?"

"About twenty years."

Now Pete was really astonished. He shook his shaggy head in disbelief. "Twenty years!? Well, Master Malcus, it's a wonder that I haven't seen you before. I've lived here for twenty-four years. Where exactly do you live in the village?"

Now the questions were starting to get a little too personal for Master Marlow. Already uncomfortable, he lowered his head and refused to speak. Seeing the master's reluctance, Felix answered for him from the front of the store.

"He lives up on the hill just on the outskirts of the village. I know everyone has always thought that that is my house, but it is actually Master Marlow's. I'm just his butler. That would make Master Marlow your best customer, Pete. Not me."

"*You're* my best customer?" he asked, looking seriously at the master.

Without looking up, Master Marlow simply

nodded. He was startled when he felt a hand slap his shoulder. He looked up. Pete was staring into his face with incredulous eyes.

"Can I just thank you, Master Malcus?" he whispered. "It's so nice to know that there is a like-minded person who shares my love of antiques. If it weren't for you, I would have gone out of business years ago."

For the first time since he had arrived at the little antique store, Master Marlow fully looked into Pete's round face. He was just as different from the rest of the world as the master was. Thick shaggy brown hair sprouted from his head. A matching bushy mustache and beard fanned out below. Tiny shrew-like eyes squinted out from beneath his thick eyebrows and smiled in the folds of his pudgy cheeks. More curls of hair stuck out at odd angles from his chest, arms, and hands. He really looked more like a sasquatch than a man! And yet, he was not ashamed of his appearance. He didn't view himself any differently from the rest of the villagers. Perhaps the master could learn to do the same.

Suddenly, Pete pointed at Master Marlow as his eyes were drawn to something about him. "That's a nice cuffed suit you've got there, Malcus. Where'd you get it?"

Master Marlow instinctively gazed down at his clothes.

"Oh, I uh…I actually made this myself."

"Really? Well, blimey! Do ya think you could make

207

me one of those? I've been wanting a new suit for my business here. I mean, I don't think these slacks and dirty old T-shirts of mine are doing my store any justice." He let out a mighty guffaw at his own expense. "Is that your occupation? Are you a tailor?"

"No, I'm not," the master replied nervously rubbing the back of his neck. "Tailoring is just uh … something I do in my spare time. I'm actually a doctor, or … I used to be anyway."

"Ya don't say," Pete muttered to himself. "We could use a doctor here. As far as I know, this village hasn't had its own doctor for more years than I've been here. They've always had a pharmacy, but what good does that do if a fellow doesn't know what he has? Most of the time, the people here use home remedies whenever they're sick. If those don't work, their only other option is to go to the hospital a few miles away, and who wants to go to the hospital to find out that they just have the common cold or something? No. What we need is a local doctor. If you're ever interested in the position, I know someone who can get you a place to open up your clinic."

"Thank you," Master Marlow softly replied, not really knowing what to think. "I'll … I'll … I'll think about it."

"I know the village would greatly appreciate your service," Pete encouraged with heart-felt sincerity.

An awkward silence suddenly drifted between the two men. The master was too amazed and confused to say anything. He was still trying to process everything that had just happened. Thankfully, Pete broke the silence with ease.

"Well, Master Malcus, it was a pleasure talking to you. I hope you'll stop by again soon. I'd love to chat some more. Oh! And do ya think you could make that suit for me?"

Not fully hearing what Pete was saying, Master Marlow simply nodded to give some kind of response.

"Thanks, pal," he said heartily as he shook Master Marlow's hand again. "Say! That's a fine cape too. I could pose for a cavalier in that."

Pete let out another roar of laughter as Felix led the dazed master toward the door. In between chuckles, Pete sputtered, "See ya, Master Felix!"

"See you later, Pete."

As they walked back down the hill, Felix turned his beaming face toward the master.

"Now see. That wasn't so bad. Was it, Sir?"

Jolted from his thoughts by Felix's voice, Master Marlow hurriedly responded, "No. No, it wasn't."

The rest of the way home, the master pondered on his experience at Knick Knacks and Knickerbockers. Different emotions were clashing within him. He couldn't believe it. After just meeting Mr. Pete for the first time, the stout owner had become his friend! What was even more astonishing to the master was the fact that Mr. Pete had not once gawked at his unsightly scars, crinkled ears, or crooked nose! He didn't seem to see his blemishes. All he saw was Master Marlow for the person he was. It was the same look that Alvera had always given him. A look that made him feel appreciated. A look that relaxed him. A look that made him feel normal.

The master's mind continued to churn. What if he did accept Pete's offer to become the village doctor? Would everyone see him as he and Alvera did? It didn't matter. Just like Alvera had told him, it only mattered what the master thought of himself. His physical deformities didn't determine who he was. His actions did. And Master Marlow wanted to help others. There was no shame in that. Let the judgmental people stare if they so wished. Master Marlow determined not to let them discourage him. Over time, they would come to appreciate what he did for them. Maybe he could help by being friendlier to others as well. Who knew? Perhaps the world had changed since the last time he had been a part of it, but he wouldn't know for sure until he exposed himself to its eyes.

CHAPTER 16

It was a sultry afternoon. The sweltering heat in the air was almost tangible with moisture. There was a slight breeze, but even its cool breath could not revive the wilting grass or the tender blossoms. Steam rose up from the ground in shimmering swirls. All around, the complaining chirps of grasshoppers and the angry hums of wasps vibrated through the air. They too were suffering under the intense heat. But even though the blistering sun beat upon her golden head and the baked dirt driveway burned her delicate feet, Alvera wasn't going to let the miserable heat of this summer afternoon spoil her excitement. Breaking into a run, she sprinted to the end of the driveway. She came to an abrupt stop when she reached the mailbox. Every day since she had left Master Marlow, Alvera had sent him a letter telling him everything that happened. So far, she had not heard back from him. Maybe today would be the day. Closing her eyes, she tentatively opened the mailbox and reached her hand inside. Halfway into the metal box, the tips of her fingers brushed the edges of an envelope. Her heart fluttered with excitement. She grabbed the paper and quickly shut the mailbox. Looking down at her hands, Alvera realized that there wasn't just one letter; there were two! One was from Felix, and the other was from Master Marlow. Alvera couldn't wait to read them till she got back inside, so she decided to open them right there at the mailbox. She read Mr. Felix's first. It read as follows:

Dearest Alvera,

Oh! How I miss you! I know you've only been gone for a few days, but it seems as if you've been gone for years! But I know no one misses you more than Master Marlow. Both the master and I have read your beautiful letters. It sounds like you have had a wonderful time being with your parents again. I know they are overjoyed to have their daughter back. But the joy you left behind in Master Marlow's life has continued to grow in him. You wouldn't believe the changes that have happened since you left! Master Marlow has been talking more to me and smiling more. He has even stopped wearing his cloak as often! He has also asked me to take down some of the heavy curtains in the windows and paint over that horrid wallpaper. But the most surprising changes of all are the appearances of mirrors and portraits in the house! I don't know where Master Marlow got all those mirrors from, but he's been hanging them up everywhere. I also got a surprise from what I saw in one of those mirrors. I had no idea just how unruly my hair had become over the years! I look like a Billy goat with this curly tuft on my chin! Then again, I have been trying to cut and comb my hair by looking at my reflection in a bowl of water for nearly twenty years. What did I expect? Anyway, enough about my hair. Like I said before, Master Marlow has also been setting out some portraits. Well, one portrait, but it's a good start. You'll never guess which picture it is. The one with the three of us in it. Master Marlow put it in a frame and set it on the mantle over the fireplace. I think he decided to place it there because the den is the main part of the house that he walks through every day. He wanted to be able to see it as often as he could. Several times, I have found him standing in front of it and smiling. I think it makes him feel like you're still with him. Consequently, the den has become a popular place for the two of us to sit and chat. I'm telling you, Alvera. I don't think that den has been used as much in all the twenty years Master Marlow has lived there as it has been used now. Oh! Alvera! I can't thank you enough for helping him! He is a better man today because of you, and both of our lives are so much happier than they used to be! Master Marlow and I can't wait to see you again! We hope that you will be able to visit us soon! Forgive me for writing so emotionally. I just miss you so much! Take care, sweet Alvera!

Your Friend,
Felix Higginshire

A huge smile glowed on Alvera's face when she finished reading Felix's letter. She was so happy for him and Master Marlow both! She always knew that the master could overcome his past, and now he had. Carefully tucking Felix's letter back into its envelope, Alvera opened Master Marlow's. He wrote the following:

Dear Alvera,

I know Felix has probably already told you in his letter, but I miss you very much. I cannot wait for you to come back and visit. I have made several changes around the house, and I would love for you to see them. However, there is one change I've made that Felix doesn't know about. I have been fixing up my secret room. By the time you come to visit, you won't even recognize it, but you will remember the portraits. I do not feel ready to set those out yet. The time will come later. For now, I am only willing to set the portrait of the three of us out. I have it placed on the mantel, so I can see your beautiful face every day. I trust you have put your copy in an equally special place. About your letters. I have been receiving them, but I apologize for not having responded to them sooner. I have been quite busy with all the changes going on, but trust me. You are no less important to me now than you were before you left. Aside from the changes occurring at home, other amazing things have been occurring elsewhere. Two days after you left, Felix forced me to accompany him into the village. I was sure that the trip would end in a disaster, but it turned out to be one of the best things that has ever happened to me. We journeyed to the antique shop, Knick Knacks and Knick-erbockers, and that is where I met Mr. Pete. He reminded me of you, Alvera. Not in appearance but in his character. He saw me as the person you always knew I could be, and I would not be that person today if it weren't for you, Alvera. Thank you for taking the time to care. But anyway, Mr. Pete told me something very interesting the day I was there. Longer than I have lived in this village, there has not been a local doctor for the people to go to. They have had to travel to the hospital several miles away, even for mild illnesses. I have thought about this long and hard, Alvera, and I did not come to my decision easily. However, I believe that it is what God would have me to do. I am going to apply for the doctor position. Being able to help you when you were injured reminded me of why I had wanted to become a doctor in the first place. To help people. I would never have been able to make such a difficult decision, however, if it weren't for you. You have taught me so much about love and trust, Alvera. Two things I never had much of in my life. I now realize that I cannot let my fears and past experiences keep me from doing what I love. It does not mat-ter what other people think of my appearance. It only mat-ters what I think of myself, and I am going to help others, even if they don't care about me. Besides, even if no one else ever accepts me, I know that you will. But I have a feeling that my attitude and disposition will help people to be more accepting of me as well. Thank you for being such a big encouragement to me. But you are not just here for me. I am also here for you. If you ever need someone to comfort you or someone to simply listen to you, you can write to me any time. As if you already haven't been doing that. Well, please be praying for me as I embark on this new adventure. I will keep you in my prayers as well. I love you dearly, Alvera. Until we meet again.

Love,
Malcus Marlow

Master Marlow's touching letter warmed Alvera's beaming heart. She hadn't realized just how important she was to him. Because of her kindness, he was finally free to pursue the life he had always wanted. And to become the doctor of his own village? Master Marlow couldn't hope to find a friendlier place. Alvera was so excited for him, but she had to admit, she missed him probably just as much as he missed her. Perhaps her parents would finally let her go visit him now that she had been home for a few days. She was eager to see all the changes the master and Felix had talked about, especially the mirrors. From what Master Marlow had said in his letter, there would be no more broken mirrors in that house. Alvera was positively bursting with joy. She just couldn't keep it to herself. Clutching the two precious letters tightly against her chest, she raced back toward her home. The hot wind rushing past her ears was like a refreshing breeze. The beads of sweat sliding down her face were cool drops of rain on her skin. Even the agitated hum of the insects had been transformed into sweet music. It was amazing how joy could change so many things in life, including a humid summer afternoon.

ABOUT THE AUTHOR

Morgan Lomax is a Christian and an Abeka Academy homeschool graduate. Ever since middle school, she has had a fervor for writing. Now she is a student at Truett McConnell University in Cleveland, Georgia and is working on her B.A. in Creative Writing and two minors: Music and the Great Commission. Aside from writing, she enjoys drawing, playing the piano, and spending time in nature. Currently, she lives in Georgia with her parents, dog, Sammie, and cat, Springs. With everything she does, Morgan hopes to glorify God with the talents He has given her.